# Summer
# of the
# Sea Monster

Raymond Coutu
Illustrated by Burgandy Beam

Rigby

*In memory of my dad,*
*Walter H. Coutu*

# Contents

Chapter One:
**My Life and Other
Natural Disasters** ...........................1

Chapter Two:
**The Legend** ................................11

Chapter Three:
**The Scheme** ..............................22

Chapter Four:
**The Barrier** ...............................33

Chapter Five:
**The Quest, Part One** ..................44

Chapter Six:
**The Setback** ..............................56

Chapter Seven:
**The Surprise** .............................67

Chapter Eight:
**The Quest, Part Two** ..................79

Chapter Nine:
**The Escape** ...............................90

Chapter Ten:
**The Last Straw** ..........................99

Chapter Eleven:
**The Conquest** ...........................105

# Chapter One

# My Life and Other Natural Disasters

*Friday evening, August 11th*

"Who's hungry?" Gabe asks as he steps through the front door and drops the pizza box on the coffee table in front of the TV.

Gabe's my stepfather. On Friday nights we always get pizza and watch a video together, usually an old disaster movie from the 1970s. Tonight it's one about a luxury liner that gets flipped upside down by a freak tidal wave. The passengers have to climb their way to safety from the top of the floating wreck to the bottom. I've seen it about a million times. It's one of Gabe's favorites. It was one of mine, too, until *my* life got flipped upside down.

Mom finds paper plates and napkins. Gabe pops the cassette into the VCR. We sit on the sofa in a row—Gabe, my mom, and me—and start eating. Mom scrapes the pepperoni off of her slice because she's pregnant and the doctor told her that too much fat isn't good for the babies. Neither of them. She's having twins.

"If they're lucky, maybe the wave will miss them this time," says Gabe. Mom chuckles. I roll my eyes.

Gabe considers himself quite a clown. And I must admit, there was a time I thought he was pretty funny. He'd do stuff like put salt in the sugar bowl or plastic bugs in the ice cube tray and wait for Mom's reaction. He'd do impressions. Or tell what-do-you-call-a-guy jokes like "What do you call a guy who's stranded in the middle of the ocean wearing a life jacket? Bob."

What do you call a kid who's stuck in on a Friday night watching another stupid disaster movie with his parents? Bored. It's not that Mom and Gabe are horrible or anything. It just bugs me that they didn't consult me before deciding to bring two more kids into this house. If they had, I would've told them that I don't want them—a brother and a sister, or a sister and a sister, or a brother and a brother. Whatever I'm going to wind up with.

We're at the part of the movie where the boat's about to go belly-up. It's New Year's Eve. Everyone's having a grand old time. Just wait, though. Their geese are cooked.

"Wonder how they filmed this scene. Like, did they use special hydraulics or something?"

Gabe asks that question every time we watch this movie. Does he really expect an answer?

"I didn't know last time and I don't know this time," I say.

He scowls at me and goes right back to the movie.

"More pizza?" Mom asks.

I nod and she slips a piece with extra cheese on my plate. I take a bite and lean into her like she's a big pillow.

Gabe and Mom have tried to get me excited about the babies by including me in all the plans, like choosing birth announcements, painting the nursery, picking names. But it isn't working. I just can't get all worked up about it the way everyone else is, like Grandpa, Aunt Louise, even my teacher from last year, Mrs. Heaney. All they talk about is what life will be like with two new babies. How wonderful it will be. Wonderful, schmonderful.

I like life just the way it is. Except for summer school, of course. Mrs. Heaney recommended I go because my reading isn't so great. So now Gabe takes me to tutoring three mornings a week, on his way to whatever house he's doing electrical work at that day.

Summer school is more fun than regular school, but not as good as surfing or skateboarding. And the only reason it's fun at all is because of Leslie, my tutor. She always manages to find better stuff to read than Mrs.

Heaney. Leslie's cool, but summer school is still school, and like I said, I'd rather be surfing or skateboarding.

Gabe hits the pause button on the remote control. "Who wants ice cream?"

"Low-fat chocolate for me," says Mom.

"With or without anchovies?" asks Mr. Comedian.

Mom looks up at him with a smile in her eyes. "With. Lots of 'em, please."

She's in a better mood than usual tonight. One of the babies is resting on a nerve in her hip, which makes walking hard for her. And complaining easy. She's anxious to have them and get on with life.

I, on the other hand, am in no hurry for the babies to arrive. It's not that I want my mom cranky and uncomfortable all the time. I just don't want newborns squawking, especially in the middle of the night. That'll make *me* cranky and uncomfortable.

"How 'bout you, sport?"

My name's Justin. "Chocolate's fine."

Mom shoots me one of her angry-mother stares. "What do you say?"

"Chocolate, *please*."

"That's better," Mom says. I rest my head on the side of her belly again and feel one of the babies kick. Already, they won't leave me alone.

As Gabe scoops the ice cream, he shouts from the kitchen, "Hey, Justin, this movie reminds me—Ted wants us to go deep-sea fishing with him this Sunday. What do you think?"

"Guess so."

Ted is one of Gabe's best customers. He lives on Rose's Island, like us, but his house is a lot bigger and fancier than ours. You can spit into the ocean from his back deck. I know, because I did it once when no one was looking.

"Guess so?" Gabe questions as he hands me my bowl. "I thought an invitation like that would send you through the ceiling.

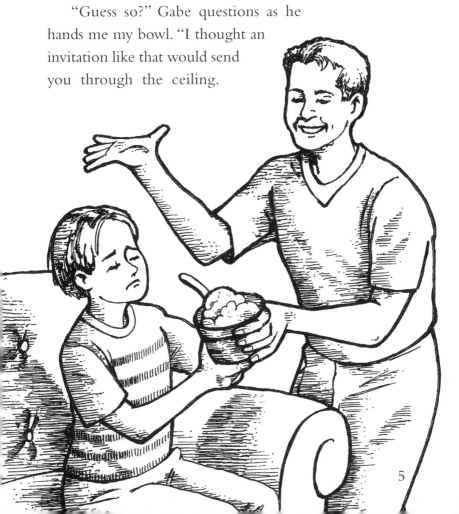

You've been bugging me to get aboard Ted's boat ever since we saw it cruise by at the beach. And all you can say is, 'Guess so'?"

"Guess so."

Gabe shakes his head. "OK, would somebody please help me out here? What happened to the real Justin LeBlanc? Clearly, this kid isn't him." He starts up the movie again.

The passengers have reached a flooded passage. Their only way out is to swim through it. Doesn't look good—that is, if you've never seen this movie before. That certainly isn't me, so I let some ice cream melt on my tongue and think about other things, like how great it would be to go fishing with Ted and Gabe on Sunday.

Ted's boat is awesome. It's 60 feet long, huge for a fishing boat. It's got a pair of 1350-horsepower engines, three staterooms with toilets *and* showers, and an entertainment center with a TV, VCR, and stereo. The best part is the flybridge, the platform above the main deck. I'm not sure why it's called that. I guess it's because you feel like you're flying when you're standing on it. I wouldn't know. Gabe's dinky boat doesn't have one.

Ted keeps his boat docked at the yacht club on the mainland, which is upriver a bit from Rose's Island. See, Rose's isn't some clump of land stuck out in the middle of the Atlantic. It's actually only a few hundred yards off-shore, connected to the mainland by a bridge. Mrs.

Heaney told us that it's called a barrier island because it's long, skinny, and runs parallel to the coast—sort of like an eight-mile-long loaf of Italian bread. The river, where Ted's yacht club is, runs past the island, directly into the Atlantic Ocean. Next stop, Portugal.

Living here is great. The public beach is right down the street from our house. That's where I windsurf, belly surf, and surf surf. But the best thing about the island is that a wildlife refuge takes up nearly two-thirds of it—the whole southern tip. There are no buildings there, only forests and marshes and creeks and coves and miles and miles of beach. Bird-watchers go there to shoot photos. Artists go there to paint. Fishermen go there to surf cast. I go there mostly to figure things out.

"How is anyone going to hear them? I mean, that hull is made of steel," says Gabe to the TV.

I don't get what he's talking about right away because I'm so caught up in my own thoughts. So I focus on the screen. We're at the part where the passengers are near the top, which is actually the bottom, and they're rapping on the ceiling, which is actually the floor, for help.

"And how did a giant wave just rise up out of nowhere in the first place? You just gotta go with it, honey," says Mom.

"The wave didn't rise up out of nowhere. An undersea earthquake caused it—7.8 on the Richter scale.

Aren't you paying attention?"

Mom shrugs and says, "Sorry."

It is amazing how wrapped up Gabe gets in these disaster movies. He got hooked on them hundreds of years ago when they were first released. Actually, it was more like 25 years ago, when he was about my age—11. He tells me all the time how much better the movies were on the big screen. How you really felt like you were on a capsized boat or in a burning building. In some movie theaters, the seats were even wired to shake when the worst happened. Now, *that's* cool. The only time our sofa shakes is when Grandpa, who weighs about 250 pounds, laughs.

Maybe I'm being a little critical tonight—about Gabe, not Grandpa. He's basically a good guy. In fact, sometimes it feels like he's my real father. Like when he drives me to tutoring or goes to teacher conferences, which was often last year because of my lousy reading. Or when I leave my backpack on the stairs and he trips over it. That's when he yells like a real father.

But Gabe's *not* my father. My father left Mom and me when I was two. I haven't heard from him since, except for the money he sends every month to help pay my way. He lives in Brooklyn, New York. That's all I know.

Mom said that marrying my dad was a big mistake, but she's glad she made it because otherwise she wouldn't have me. They just never got along. She says that she was too young to be a wife back then. And my dad was too selfish to be a husband. She always tells me that their split-up had nothing to do with me.

I have my doubts, though. Sometimes I think she says that to make me feel better. And her feel less guilty. I love my mom, but she doesn't always make the best decisions. Like hooking up with Gabe and deciding to have twins before talking to me about it. Like painting the house "mauve." It's pink.

Mom pulls me closer and gives me a quick kiss on the top of my head. "You OK, Justin?" she asks, as if she knows what I'm thinking.

"I'm fine," I tell her.

Mom married Gabe about three years after my dad left. Gabe and I didn't hit it off at first because he had never really been around kids before. He'd never lived with them or worked with them or anything, so he didn't know how to talk to me. He would ask stuff like, "Would you like to go to the playground today?" stretching out the words like I was a baby or something. I was actually five and in kindergarten at the time.

But I eventually set him straight. Before long we were riding bikes together and playing computer games. Talking about important things like ant farms.

Lately, though, he's been getting on my nerves, kinda the way he did when he first started coming around. But now it's not his baby talk that's driving me crazy. It's his babies, period. Both of them. Why are he and Mom messing up a good thing? Flipping our lives up-side down?

The video's over and the credits are rolling.

"What a movie. A classic. Definitely my favorite," Gabe says with a big grin.

Six passengers survived . . . again. What a surprise. Hope I wind up so lucky.

# Chapter Two

# The Legend

*Monday morning, August 14th*

The sun's out, it's 90 degrees, and, like I said, the beach is only two seconds from my house. But where am I? At summer school. What's wrong with this picture?

My tutor Leslie and I meet on Mondays, Wednesdays, and Fridays. Today's Monday, and like every Monday, she starts the session by asking, "How was the weekend, Justin?"

"It was OK."

"Just OK?"

I nod and flip through the reader's journal that I'm supposed to be keeping but don't.

"What did you do?"

I really don't want to answer. I'd rather just get this session over with as soon as possible. But I can't blame Leslie for being friendly, so I throw her a bone. "Went deep-sea fishing with Gabe and one of his customers."

"Did you catch anything?"

"A 4-foot bluefish."

"That sounds like fun," Leslie says, like she's trying to convince me it was.

"It was OK." I don't look up from the empty pages of my journal.

"Guess the question is, are *you* OK?"

"I'm fine," I lie. "Can we read?"

"Ah, the question every teacher dreams of hearing, but I thought we'd start with a spelling quiz," Leslie says.

I glare at her.

She nudges my left arm with her elbow and grins. "Just kidding. I knew that would get a rise out of you."

Leslie definitely knows what ticks me off. And what makes me tick. She talks to me like a real person. Like when I do a good job, she doesn't just say, "Good job." She tells me why, and that makes it easier to do it again. It makes me *want* to do it again. Most of the other teachers I've had haven't been so quick to point out what I do right. But they've been like jackrabbits when it comes to telling me what I do wrong.

It's as if Leslie can see inside my head. Unscramble everything and help me make sense of it, kinda like my best friend, Kate, only different. Kate's a kid, and kids are supposed to be able to figure out what other kids are thinking. To listen in ways no adult can, or will. To be honest. Those are the things kids do best . . . except for Tony Morrow who stole my skateboard last year, but that's another story.

No, Leslie is different. Different from Kate, different from other grown-ups. She makes me feel OK about myself. She makes me feel, well—not exactly smart, but not stupid. Sometimes she helps me find answers to questions before I even ask them, like she's psychic or something. Like why seeing a big word in a book stops me dead. Why keeping track of a lot of characters is so hard for me. And why Gabe's jokes aren't as funny as they used to be.

But today I just don't feel like talking about it.

"Since you liked that magazine article on the abominable snowman so much, I thought we might give this a try." Leslie pulls a book from her shoulder bag and hands it to me. *Bigfoot: Fact or Fiction?* by Malcolm Norman. Looks promising.

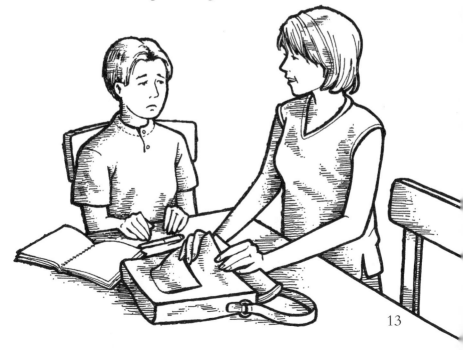

I've always been interested in unexplained stuff—UFOs, ghost sightings, lost civilizations like Atlantis. I'm not sure why. I think it has something to do with the fact that all the answers aren't there yet. And that scientists aren't really the ones who are looking for answers. Average people are, too, like Lhakpa Dolma, the Nepalese kid who first spotted the abominable snowman, according to the magazine article I read. I mean, when the experts don't take this stuff seriously, the door's wide open for everyone else. Maybe *I'll* be the average-person-off-the-street who discovers Atlantis, contacts Martians, or unlocks the secrets of the universe. Imagine that.

I flip through the Bigfoot book. There are lots of cool pictures and not too, too many words. Only 51 pages. Leslie tells me to skim the back cover to decide if it's a book I really want to read. Then she tells me to look over the table of contents to get a feel for the author's ideas and how he organizes them.

I give the book a nod and we start in. Leslie asks me to read the first few pages out loud while she makes notes on the pad that she always keeps at her side. I think it's attached to her by magnets or something.

I like reading to Leslie, but we don't always do it this way. Sometimes she reads to me. Sometimes we read silently together and then talk about the story. Sometimes we write about it. Sometimes we don't read at all; we just play word games.

Don't get me wrong. I don't hate regular school. Actually, there were tons of good things about Mrs. Heaney, like the way she let us use uncooked macaroni to figure out math problems. But with her, reading always felt like work. With Leslie, it feels like work, too, but fun work. It's hard to explain. I guess that's what makes Leslie special.

The book starts with a story about Albert Postman, a guy who was kidnapped by Bigfoot while camping. Albert was just snoring away when all of a sudden some dude came along, stuffed him deeper into his sleeping bag, and dragged him off. Next morning, he found himself surrounded by Bigfoot's family: two adults, a baby, and a medium-sized one. They didn't hurt him, just kept him prisoner—or so he claimed. On the sixth day, Bigfoot ate something he shouldn't have from Albert's pack. Huge mistake. That ape wound up sick as a dog, and Albert escaped.

Leslie has me tell the story in my own words, jots down a couple of notes, and asks if I think Albert's story is true.

"Sure," I say.

"What makes you so sure, Justin?"

"The book says so."

"Does it?"

That's Leslie's code for sending me back in. I flip pages looking for a clue that Albert isn't just telling a tall tale, but I come up empty. "Maybe it isn't true."

"What's missing?" she asks.

I think long and hard about it. This is the "work" part of fun work. "Proof?"

"Exactly! Let's read on to find out if there's any evidence that Bigfoot exists."

Sure enough, the book is awesome. I finished over half of it and understood every bit. Score another one for Leslie. It had tons of other stories about Bigfoot sightings, as well as evidence that he's real, like photos, tape recordings, and plaster casts of gigantic footprints. It even showed stills from a movie shot by Roger Patterson in 1967 of Bigfoot walking into the woods and looking right into the camera! Gabe and I will have to look for that video at Movie Mart.

But, as usual with this stuff, the scientists aren't convinced. They think people like Patterson are just out to make a buck or get famous. I'm not so sure. Those pictures look awfully convincing to me.

"Maybe I'll find Bigfoot around here," I tell Leslie. "Prove those scientists wrong."

"I think you'd be wasting your time."

I look at Leslie out of the corner of one eye. "What makes *you* so sure?"

She taps the cover of the book, which reminds me of what I read. So far, Bigfoot has only been spotted in the Pacific Northwest, about a million miles from Rose's Island. "You may be right." I admit.

"That's not to say that we don't have our own mysterious creatures."

"Whattaya mean?"

"Haven't you heard about Old Orchard?"

That's a coastal town about an hour north of here, in Maine. But we're not talking about towns. We're talking about monsters. "Old Orchard?"

"The sea monster," says Leslie. "Back in 1905, a creature—half fish, half lizard—washed up on Old Orchard Beach and was discovered by a guy named F. E. Sidelinger."

"How do you know so much?"

"I read," she says, then goes on. "It floated in one night at high tide—dead. Next morning, Mr. Sidelinger spotted it on the beach and pointed it out to a few other strollers. Before long, hundreds of people came to get a peek."

"What did it look like?"

"About 150 feet long with no teeth, tiny legs, a 15-foot tongue with a neck to match. Oh, and eyes the size of watermelons."

*My* eyes get about as big as watermelons. "More. Tell me more."

"Well, Mr. Sidelinger wasn't a scientist, but he was a pretty sharp guy with a real interest in the extraordinary. Sort of like you, only taller and with a mustache. When he saw how wild the public was about seeing the sea monster, he chopped off its head and put it on display in a tent. People paid good money to go inside, even though it stank to high heaven."

"Why only the head?"

"I guess the rest of it was too big to carry."

"What happened to the rest of it?" I ask. "Is it in a museum somewhere?"

"I don't know about that. But I do know this: Mr. Sidelinger performed an autopsy on . . . well . . . the rest of it."

"Autopsy?"

"He cut it open and looked inside."

"What did he find?"

"A heart the size of a barrel, lungs, and some baby sea monsters. Apparently, Old Orchard was a girl sea monster."

This is all too much. Even I, Justin LeBlanc, believer in all things unbelievable, know a rat when I smell one. "Where's your evidence?"

Leslie chuckles, like I caught her at her own game. She nudges me to slide down the table to the computer terminal at the other end. "Type this Web site address in," she says. Then she rattles off something that sounds like her tongue got stuck on a few letters.

"Say what?" I ask, like she's crazy.

She repeats the string of letters, then adds, "It's a Web site about cryptozoologists and their work."

"Cryptozoologists?"

She writes the word on a page in her notepad. "Try to figure it out. Look at the parts. I know you know at least one of them."

At first I think this is no time for a vocabulary lesson, but then I remember that I *am* in summer school, so maybe it is.

Leslie and I do this sort of thing a lot, actually. It's kind of fun—especially when I can spot more little words inside the big word than she thinks I can.

"I see two: 'zoologist,'—animal scientist, and 'crypt,'—the place where dead people get stashed. Gabe and I watched a video once, *It Came from the Crypt.* That's how I know."

"You and Gabe watch too many videos. You should be reading more."

"Yeah, yeah." I've heard that one before.

"So 'cryptozoologist' must mean something like 'dead animal scientist.'"

Leslie points to different parts of the word. "Well, you got the animal scientist part right, but notice that 'crypt' has an *o* after it. It's not just 'crypt'; it's 'crypto.' Let's look it up." In Leslie-speak, that means *I* look it up.

I pull the dictionary from the shelf above the computer, flip to *c*, and find it: "crypto-: secret, of obscure origin, from Greek *kruptos*, hidden."

"Got it," I say. "It means secret, obscure animal scientist."

"Close, but I think the 'secret and obscure' part refers more to the animal than to the scientist."

"Secret, obscure animals?"

"Yes. A cryptozoologist is an expert who studies mysterious creatures. Creatures whose existence hasn't been proven by scientists—like Bigfoot and Old Orchard."

"They actually pay people to do that?" I'm excited. This could be the start of something really, really big. My future. My key to unlocking the secrets of the universe.

"They do. But it's hard work, I'm sure. Cryptozoologists have to read and research, write and lecture, like any scholar. It's not just about hanging out in the woods and waiting for Bigfoot to snatch you up in your sleeping bag. Here, check this out. "

Leslie takes us to a Web site. It's definitely one for grown-ups—too many words, not enough pictures—but I'm not about to let that scare me. She does a search for "Old Orchard," and we learn more about Mr. Sidelinger's find. Turns out the scientists passed Old Orchard off as a blue whale because of the way Sidelinger described her in a pamphlet he published about his discovery.

However, there were a few things about Old Orchard that stumped the scientists—like her tiny head and feet, her watermelon eyes, and her long neck. Whales have big heads, tiny eyes, and no necks or feet. So maybe she wasn't a whale after all. Maybe those scientists just needed to sound smart, like they had all the answers. Maybe they were just too spooked by the possibility that sea monsters really might exist.

While I'm gazing out the window, thinking about Old Orchard, I see Mom pull up in the big old car Grandpa gave her when he moved into the assisted-living complex. Her belly's touching the steering wheel. Session's over.

Leslie looks me in the eye, squeezes my shoulder, and says, "Excellent reading today, my friend. Keep it up," like she means it. That makes me feel good. Really good. A lot better than I did when I got here. Maybe even good enough to write something in my reader's journal tonight. After all, like Leslie said, writing's one of the things cryptozoologists do, so if I'm going to be one, I need to get started.

# Chapter Three

# The Scheme

***Monday afternoon and evening, August 14th***

I love to drift. In fact, that's what Kate and I are doing right now, drifting in our inner tubes in one of the wildlife refuge's creeks. The sun's beating down on us, making me feel like a bagel in the toaster oven.

"Did you know that without the sun, life as we know it wouldn't exist?" Kate asks.

"No, I didn't," I answer, only half interested.

"It's true. Without the sun, there would be no solar radiation. And without solar radiation, there would be no rain or air. And without rain or air, there would be no life."

Kate's really smart. She thinks some more, then looks at me over the top of her sunglasses. "Did you put on sunblock?"

Smart—and bossy. "Who are you, my mother?" I respond.

With that, I suddenly feel something land on my stomach. It's Kate's SPF30. "Thanks, Mom." I slather some on and throw the tube onto the creek bank.

I know it's weird for a guy to have a girl as his best friend, but I don't have much choice living on Rose's Island. Fact is, there aren't too many kids here. Most of them live in subdivisions on the mainland. Kate lives two streets over, on Piper Way. She's not like other girls, who can't tell a Bigfoot from a Yeti, a swordfish from a marlin. She's interested in everything.

But that's a cop-out. Sure, Kate is different from most girls, but it's a two-way street. Sometimes I feel different from most guys. I'd get creamed for saying this at school, but I find them kinda boring. I mean, all they talk about is skateboards and pro wrestling and rap music. I like some of that stuff, but life is bigger. And Kate knows it. That's one reason we're friends.

"How was Ted's boat yesterday?" she asks.

"Excellent. He let me steer for a whole half hour, even through the channel. Then we fished all afternoon."

"Did you catch anything?"

"Bluefish, 4-foot."

"Liar."

Oh well, at least Leslie had fallen for it.

Another reason Kate and I are friends is because our mothers are friends, too. They spent summers on Rose's Island as kids. Played together, just like Kate and me. I don't remember a time when Kate wasn't around. I even have this fuzzy memory of her in diapers. I remind her of that when I need to get a rise out of her.

Both our houses used to be summer cottages with no heat or insulation, but we turned them into year-round homes over the past ten years. Gabe did most of the work on ours.

A lot of newcomers live in overhauled cottages, too. Or they've torn down the cottages completely and built bigger homes for a better view, like Ted did. But the difference between the newcomers and us old-timers is that they don't think about what they're losing, just what they're getting. It's kind of sad. To me, living in a place means more than looking out your window and seeing the ocean. It means really knowing it—every inch of it.

I remember a joke I just heard from Gabe. Kate will never get this one. "What do you call a guy who forgets to open his fireplace flue?"

"Smokey."

Man, she's smart.

"Now tell me something I don't know," she says.

"A sea monster washed up on Old Orchard Beach."

"Yeah, right. And Elvis is playing at my 12th birthday party."

"I'm serious." This time it's me looking at her like I know it all.

Kate looks back. "A sea monster?"

I tell her the whole story just the way I remember it, right down to the watermelon eyes. And I must've done a good job because Kate's hooked.

"It does sound suspicious," she admits.

"Suspicious is putting it lightly. Do you know how big the ocean is? Those scientists can't know everything that's going on down there."

"But, you know, the scientists might've been right," says Kate. "Maybe it

*was* a blue whale. I mean, it was the right size. And whales are spotted now and then off the Maine coast."

"A blue whale with huge eyes, a skinny neck, and legs? As if," I spit back.

"Besides, that Sidelinger sounds like a shady guy to me, like he might've been in it for the money."

Kate is slipping into sensible, no-fun mode, like she has a habit of doing. Something must be done about it immediately. I hop off my tube and dog-paddle up to hers, my eyes peeking out above the water's surface, buggy like a giant frog's. "Who knows what lurks beneath . . . ?" I whisper in a throaty voice.

And with that, I dive under and grab one side of her tube. She tries to get away and falls off. She squeals, takes a deep breath, and goes under.

We start splashing and diving, diving and splashing, unable to breathe not because we're submerged most of the time, but because we're laughing so hard.

Finally, we pull ourselves back onto our tubes. We need the rest.

"I'll get my dad to take me to the aquarium this weekend," Kate says after she catches her breath. "He's got a friend there, Richard, who's in charge of educational programs. He'll be able to figure it out."

Reason number three Kate and I are friends: Her parents are divorced, too. But Kate sees her dad all the time. She stays with him two weekends a month at his place in Boston. She's lucky. He lives in a ritzy old building. She has her own room with a marble fireplace and a chandelier in it. And she gets to go to places like the science museum and the aquarium when she's visiting because they're all nearby, right on the subway. Guess that's why she's so smart.

"We don't need Richard," I say. We can figure it out ourselves, Kate. We'll do a little research . . . and catch a sea monster."

"Are you nuts?"

"No, I'm a future cryptozoologist."

"Excuse me?"

Finally I know something she doesn't. "A guy who studies creatures whose existence hasn't been proven." I let that sink in for a moment. "It comes from the Greek word for hidden, *kruptos.*"

"I knew that."

"Now who's the liar?" I splash her.

Kate splashes back and then asks, "Wouldn't it be easier just to ask Richard?"

"Listen, until we come up with some evidence, this is between you and me. I don't want anyone, especially some brain from the aquarium, snooping around, looking to get in on our good thing."

" 'Good thing'? There is no good thing—just your crazy fantasy."

"It's not a fantasy. I know there's a sea monster out

there. I know it."

"OK, Mr. Cryptozoologist, tell me, how do you plan on luring him in? And then proving that you did? After all, Sidelinger had it easy. The thing was just lying there on the beach, practically begging him to chop off its head, show it off, and make a million bucks."

"First, that's *Dr.* Cryptozoologist to you. Second, I've been fishing longer than I've been blowing my own nose, so I think I know a thing or two about getting what I want from the ocean."

"Say you find a sea monster—would you keep it?"

"No. I'm going to shoot a video that'll set the world's heads spinning, just like Roger Patterson did when he caught Bigfoot taking a Sunday stroll. Then I'll let it go."

Kate looks at me like she's not sure if I'm brilliant or bonkers. And, honestly, I'm feeling kind of the same way about myself.

"You *are* the best fisherman I know," she admits.

"Won the derby three years straight."

"For your age group."

"Doesn't matter—I won. Those competitions and others. And I've got a slew of trophies to prove it. I'm telling you, if anyone knows what it takes to catch a sea monster, it's me. Are you in?"

"Fine," Kate says. "I don't know why I'm saying this, but I'm in."

"See you at Scrub Point tomorrow, two o'clock sharp. Don't be late."

After dinner, I go to the library to do a little research. I want to find out what kind of animal Old Orchard is since that will help me decide what kind of bait to use. But that's not my only reason for this trip. I also need to get away from the folks.

Mom got a picture of the babies today, not like one taken at a studio, of course, since they aren't born yet. It's a weird, grainy picture taken with a special camera that shoots through skin. It's called an ultrasound. Anyway, you can't really make them out too much. The picture isn't very clear. Gabe and Mom are all gaga about them, saying how cute they are. Saying how much they look like Gabe. I *had* to get out of there.

So here I am, at the library. Leslie would be proud. Problem is, I don't know how to use the library very well. I've never had a good reason to before. Oh sure, I've had book reports and science projects and stuff, but in my opinion, those have always been somebody else's idea of a good reason. Not mine.

When the librarian sees me standing there looking like a lost kid at the supermarket, she walks over and asks, "Do you need some help?"

I don't want to tell her what I'm up to. When you're on the verge of something this big, no one can be trusted. Even friendly librarians.

"I'm doing a report on amphibians for summer school," I tell her. I figure amphibians is a good place to start, since Old Orchard had legs. Tiny ones, but definitely legs. So she wasn't a fish, that's for sure.

The librarian finds me a book about amphibians, and we open it up together on one of the big tables. "Are you interested in a particular kind of amphibian?" she asks. "It says there are three categories: frogs and toads, salamanders, and caecilians."

Think, think, think. I have no idea what a caecilian is, so that one's out. And Old Orchard sure didn't look like a frog or toad. "Salamanders," I tell her, sounding a lot more confident than I am.

The librarian flags the chapter on salamanders, finds me another book, a couple of magazine articles, and a Web site about amphibians. "That ought to get you started. If you have any questions, just ask."

I thank her and stare at the pile. There's a lot to cover, and I have to be home in a half hour. So much for those time-management skills Leslie's always nagging me about.

So I dig in. First I look at the pictures and check the captions, figuring maybe I can find out what I need to know without actually doing a lot of reading. There are a few different species of salamander, and most of them fit Old Orchard's description: tiny head and legs, big eyes, no teeth. Their long tails stump me, though.

I don't remember Leslie saying anything about Old Orchard having a tail . . . but all sea monsters have tails, right?

I decide I have to do some reading. So I let my finger run across the sentences, waiting for words like "habitat," "size," and "feeding habits" to jump out at me and writing down what might be useful.

Turns out, most salamanders divide their time between land and water, which explains why they look so much like a cross between a lizard and a fish. They're carnivores. They eat bugs and slugs and stuff, which reminds me of the time Tony Morrow ate a live beetle on a dare.

I find a section in the book called "Mammoth Amphibians," which tells me that the giant salamander is the biggest of all living amphibians. It hardly ever leaves the water, and it breathes with lungs. Just like Old Orchard, I think, feeling my hands shake and my heart thump against my T-shirt. Feeling like I'm onto something.

Then I get to the last sentence: "The giant salamander can reach $5\frac{1}{4}$ feet in length." Big deal. Old Orchard was supposedly 150 feet long.

At first I'm bummed out, like maybe I'm headed down a dead end, but then I start thinking. Maybe Old Orchard was some sort of mutant salamander. Maybe some molecular shift in the environment or a nasty chemical spill changed that tiny salamander's genetic structure and turned it into the monster that is . . . or was . . . Old Orchard.

I scribble like crazy until I hear the grandfather clock in the corner strike 8:00. I'm late again. I didn't get to half the stuff the librarian gave me, and I don't even have time to check any of the references out. So I finish writing my last sentence—"Get meat"—and dash out, figuring that I have all the information I need, anyway. Figuring that that monster will be mine in no time.

# Chapter Four

# The Barrier

*Tuesday morning, August 15th*

Morning TV is so lame. On this show, for example, they're giving a report on making beauty products from stuff lying around the house—like facial scrub from kitty litter. I've got a strong stomach, but this isn't helping me keep my cereal down. I start channel surfing.

Just when I find something important enough to stop for, Mom walks into the kitchen in her purple bathrobe. She looks like a big, blond Easter egg.

"Good morning," she says. Her voice sounds like sandpaper.

"Morning," I say back, slurping down the leftover milk in my bowl without taking my eyes off the set.

Mom puts the kettle on for herb tea because the doctor says that coffee, like fat, is bad for the babies. "Did you sleep OK?" she asks.

"Yep." I always sleep OK the night before I don't have tutoring. Although Leslie is the best teacher I've ever had, I still get nervous when I have to read. After all, I've only known Leslie for about two months, but I've struggled with reading for five years. Sometimes thinking about it keeps me awake.

Like the other night, I had a nightmare. In it, I took a book off a shelf and opened it. But all the words looked like they were in another language—maybe French. And then a teacher—maybe Mrs. Connelly from third grade—said to me in some weird, mechanical tone, "Justin, read for the class." I turned around and saw all the kids staring at me. Waiting. I woke up and couldn't get back to sleep.

"Did *you* sleep OK?" I ask, suddenly realizing that I'm stuck on myself.

"Not really. The twins were practicing their swimming all night." She clutches her middle and sits down at the table with me. "I have no doubt they'll be bringing home Olympic gold within six months. I just hope I'm alive to share their glory."

Mom can be funny, like Gabe. I think that's partly why she hooked up with him. They made each other laugh. And when they met, she needed a laugh bad. I mean, there she was, raising me all alone, making paper-route wages as an office manager for a real estate company downtown.

Brenda (Kate's mother) and my grandparents helped as much as they could, but they had their own problems. Brenda was alone, too, with a kid to bring up. And Grandma and Grandpa were old.

My grandparents watched me when Mom wasn't around. For a while she went out a lot at night with her girlfriends. Sometimes, after she got home, she'd come into my bedroom and stare at me while I pretended to sleep. Then she'd lean over and kiss me on the cheek. I don't know what she was thinking during those night-time visits, but whatever it was, it scared me. I thought she might leave, just like my father did. And that those kisses were her way of saying good-bye.

I lose myself in the TV show again, but still feel Mom's eyes on me. "That's going to fry your brain, you know," she says.

I ignore her.

"Hello," she calls, waving her hands like she's trying to get my attention in a crowd.

I slide my eyes in her direction. "Can I help you?"

"You watch too much TV, Justin."

"Who put the TV in the kitchen in the first place?"

"I put it here to watch the news. And cooking shows so I could prepare delicious, nutritious meals for you. Like a good mother."

I look at her now. "Mom, we've had take-out the last three nights."

She turns to the chair next to me, as if there's a person in it. "My stomach is rumbling like an alien is about to burst from it, and he expects gourmet cooking."

"Not gourmet, just something that doesn't come from a paper bag."

Maybe I shouldn't have said that. I was only kidding anyway. I *like* fast food. Anyway, Mom's eyes turn to slits, and she looks out the window. I guess she could use a laugh right now. Where's Gabe when you need him?

Mom started going out with Gabe about the time we found out Grandma was sick. Mom met Gabe at her office; he was doing some work on a house that her company was about to put up for sale. While they were dating, they'd have these big, behind-the-door conversations that I couldn't really hear. I'd press my ear to the door and listen as hard as I could, but all I'd get was the sound of their voices, not their words. Sometimes I'd hear Mom crying—about Grandma, I suppose—and that would frighten me. But within minutes, Gabe would have her laughing. He *always* made her laugh. They made each other laugh.

Now Mom turns back to me. "You know, you're old enough to cook, Justin. If you want a real meal, why don't you make it?"

"Maybe I will."

The kettle starts whistling, and not a minute too soon. The conversation's moving in a bad direction. Mom must sense it herself because she changes the subject. "Let's do something today," she says, pouring hot water into the mug Aunt Louise brought her back from Ireland.

"Like what?"

"It's gorgeous out. Brenda's not working. Maybe she and Kate would want to hang out." Brenda is a waitress at a restaurant on the river, just down from Ted's yacht club. People come all the way from Boston to go there—and spend way too much on fish that I can get for the cost of bait.

"And do what?" I ask.

Mom thinks. "How about a picnic at Lighthouse Point? We haven't done that for a while."

No way. Kate and I already have beach plans at two o'clock today—at Scrub Point, the island's southernmost tip. But I can't tell Mom that because of all the poison ivy down there. See, last fall I was out of school for two weeks with the worst case Dr. Mitchell had seen in ten years. I started breaking out right after an afternoon at Scrub Point. Since then, Kate and I have learned how to avoid the poison ivy. We just stick to the boardwalk until we hit the beach. But Mom still has a fit every time I go there.

Of all places, why did she have to suggest the beach? Then again, this *is* an island. What do I tell her?

"I just remembered, Mom. I've got plans."

"What kind of plans?"

My mind is blank. Of course it's not just where I'm going that's a secret, but also *why*. I don't want Mom or any other grown-up—including some brain from the aquarium—to know that Kate and I are hunting sea monsters. They'll just mess up our plan by telling us what we can or can't do, or how to do it better. That's the last thing we need. Once we catch that sea monster and videotape it, I'll share everything with them. The whole story.

Just when I'm about to say something stupid, something that would get me into hot water, Gabe walks in and saves me. He's all scrubbed, dressed, and ready for work, as usual. "Good morning," he sings out.

What makes him so cheerful in the morning? So energized? He *is* an electrician, I suppose. Maybe it has something to do with sticking his fingers into outlets all day. He fills a bowl with cereal, grabs a spoon from the drawer, and joins us at the table.

He must notice how terrible Mom looks because he says, "Bad night?"

"Of the living dead."

"Only about 20 more days to go." Gabe points toward the calendar on the wall. He's been marking off the days to Mom's due date, September 4th, using little teddy bear stickers. September 4th is Labor Day, and they think it's a hysterical coincidence that she could go into labor on Labor Day. To me, Labor Day just means going back to school.

"Can a person survive 20 days without sleep?" Mom asks.

"You'll sleep. You just had a lousy night," Gabe says, squeezing her upper arm. "You know, you'll probably lose even more sleep after they're here."

She stares at him like he doesn't know what he's talking about. "I don't think so."

"Why?"

"Because you'll be there to help out, Mr. Mom, especially in the middle of the night. We're a team, remember?"

"I remember. Consider me the quarterback," Gabe says.

More like the water boy, I think. Gabe's got a lot to learn about bringing up babies. Thankfully, Mom's been through it once and can show him the ropes.

They must sense that I'm not into the conversation, because, out of nowhere, Gabe asks what I'm up to today. That happens a lot. They get all wrapped up in talking about the twins, and then suddenly they realize they already *have* a kid, and they toss me some stupid question.

"I dunno."

"You said you had plans," Mom says.

Oops. How did we find our way back to this conversation? "Oh yeah, I do." I panic for a moment, but then the perfect story comes to me. "I told George I'd pull traps with him."

George is a guy who lives on the mainland, a retired lawyer with a lobster boat. I go out with him sometimes and help collect his catch.

"That's nice of you. George isn't getting any younger," Mom says.

"I hope he's not getting any cheaper, either," Gabe grumbles. "He is paying you, right?"

"Oh, sure," I mumble, trying to think of a way to change the subject before I end up telling a million lies.

"Fair?"

"Fair enough."

"How much is 'fair enough'?"

Mom must be feeling the same way I do, which doesn't surprise me. She hates talking about money because it always leads to arguments. So she says, "I forgot to ask—how was tutoring yesterday?"

"Fine," I say.

"What did Leslie have you read?"

"A book."

Mom and Gabe look at each other like they'd like to say something but won't. "What book, honey?" Mom asks calmly, but with an edge.

I'm not sure whether to tell them. They might get suspicious. But I can't think of another subject, and I've already lied to them once this morning, so I take a chance. "A book about Bigfoot."

"That sounds interesting," Mom says.

"It was OK."

"You know, I once saw a Bigfoot," Gabe comments.

Finally, something worth listening to. I perk up, but not too much. I don't want him thinking I like him as much as I used to. "You did?"

"Yep."

"Where?"

"On the beach."

That doesn't make sense to me, but I'm not ruling anything out at this point. "Bigfoot lives in the woods."

"Not this one. It was my Uncle Frank's footprint. He has the biggest feet I've ever seen. He's gotta wear about size 13s."

Mom cracks up. "I get it. Big foot!"

Now they're both laughing, tears streaming down their faces. I just sit there with my arms crossed. "That's not funny," I say. "You know, there are scientists out there who study this stuff. They're called cryptozoologists."

Their laughter dies down. "More like 'crazy-olo-gists,'" says Gabe.

I look him straight in the eye. "You wouldn't call a scientist crazy if he was looking for life on Mars, would you? Why is he crazy if he's looking for Bigfoot?"

"Those guys are just out to make a buck, Justin. To get written up in the tabloids."

I tell him about Roger Patterson, about how some scientists thought his film was a fake but couldn't prove it. Even they had to admit that guys in gorilla costumes don't walk that way. But Gabe doesn't buy it.

"I've seen that footage, Justin. It's totally manufactured. I'm telling you, Roger and his buddy were just bored and looking for something that would get people talking. And it did."

I try to come up with a sensible argument, but it's

too late—just being around Gabe is making *me* crazy. "What do *you* know?"

Mom cuts in. "Honey, Gabe might be right. Those men weren't scientists."

I'm boiling. "And neither is he," I say, motioning toward Gabe. "But he seems to know everything."

"He's just being realistic," says Mom, as if that's supposed to help me or something.

"Why do you always take his side? Why can't *I* be right for a change?"

Then Gabe cuts in. "Calm down."

Wrong thing to say. "Don't tell me what to do," I mutter.

Now he's mad. "I'll tell you whatever I want to tell you."

I get up from the table so fast that the chair falls onto the floor. Then I run upstairs to my bedroom and slam the door. I sit on the floor and try to clear my head, ignoring the knocks on the door. I hear the sound of Gabe and Mom's voices, but not their words. No one's laughing now, and I don't care.

Why can't they think about something—no, some-one—other than themselves and those babies? Why can't they see things my way? Be willing to believe that I know what I'm talking about? I'm stuck with the worst parents any kid ever had.

Then I stop, take a deep breath and remind myself that there are more important things in life—like catching that sea monster.

After awhile the knocks stop, and I hear Gabe leave for work. Don't know what Mom's doing now—probably washing the dishes or throwing in a load of laundry. She knows there's no point in talking to me when I'm upset. And she knows I'll feel guilty and apologize to Gabe.

And I probably will. But not right away. I'll be busy unlocking the secrets of the universe. And I start this afternoon.

# Chapter Five

# The Quest, Part One

*Tuesday afternoon, August 15th*

It takes a little while to recover from my rotten mood, but I do. Pedaling my bike as fast as I can helps. The bad stuff is like a baseball cap—it doesn't stand a chance of staying on once I hit a certain speed.

I'm on my way to meet Kate, not paying much attention to where I'm going because I've ridden this route so many times. The road is long and straight. Scrub Point is at the very end. If I wind up in the ocean, I'll know I've gone too far.

I'm all loaded down with equipment—rods, tackle box, video camera, and a red helium balloon tied to my handlebars. I must look like some weird parade float. I'm wearing my lucky fishing T-shirt, too, the one that says "Harrison's." That's where Gabe and I buy our bait and dock our dinky boat. I've worn this shirt to every derby

I've won. And I've never washed it 'cause I'm afraid all the luck will go down the drain with the dirt. Sure, I stink like a three-day-old perch when I have it on, but I don't care because that's what real fishermen are supposed to smell like.

It's not the best time of day for surfcasting. Most serious fishermen are out at the crack of dawn, or a couple of hours before sunset, but what can I do? Mom and Gabe would definitely know something's up if I turned up missing at those times.

The conditions aren't great for surfcasting, either. The wind is blowing offshore, toward the ocean, meaning game fish are way out—and sea monsters probably are, too. See, an onshore wind—that's a wind coming *from* the ocean—kicks up the waves. That churns up natural bait on the bottom, which brings hungry game fish in close to the beach. So the best time to surfcast is after a big storm, when the waves are humongous. Feeding activity tends to get wild! In fact, I've heard about swordfish just flopping ashore, sort of like Old Orchard, except alive.

But onshore wind or no onshore wind, bad timing or no bad timing, I'm not worried, because I've got a plan. If that monster doesn't want to pick up his dinner, no problem. I deliver.

I reach the end of the 8-mile road without winding up in the ocean. Kate's waiting for me. I check my fake diver's watch. It's two o'clock, right on the nose.

"You're early," I tell her, so she knows I'm on time.

"I'm always early, but you never know that because you're always late."

"Not today," I say, lifting the backpack off of my shoulders and hopping off the bike.

"What's with the balloon?" asks Kate.

"I like balloons."

"Yeah, sure. You've got something up your sleeve."

"You're a smart cookie," I tell her. Fishing is one of the few things where I know more than Kate. "Yes, I do have something up my sleeve. But I'm afraid that's where it's going to stay until we're on the beach and all my tools are organized."

"What do you think you are, a surgeon?"

"Cryptozoologist."

Kate's eyes say, "give me a break," but I ignore her. We wheel our bikes to the rack and lock them up. Then we divvy up the supplies. I hand Kate the tackle box. The sand spikes—fishing rod holders that look a little like giant candlesticks—are tied across my handlebars, along with the balloon. I cut the strings with my gutting knife, careful not to send the balloon soaring.

"Did Gabe say you could use his fishing equipment?" Kate asks.

"No. But what he doesn't know won't bother him."

46

"Don't be so sure. You know how he is about his stuff, Justin. He guards it with his life."

"Not when he's at work."

Kate rests the two sand spikes on her left shoulder, and for balance picks up the tackle box with her right hand. "OK, but remember I warned you," she says, turning and heading for the boardwalk that leads to the beach.

I grab the rest of the stuff and follow. I'm watching every step because this is the section I mentioned earlier, the one filled with poison ivy. I can see the shiny leaves licking the edges of the boardwalk and looking hungry. So I walk carefully, one foot directly in front of the other to avoid their bite.

All fear evaporates when I reach the end of the boardwalk and spot the water: a big blanket of blues, all sparkly in the sunshine. That's right, "blues" with an *s*— all different kinds—gray ones and green ones and even purple ones. You need to look really close to notice the colors, but they're there. I never knew that there were so many different blues until I started looking really close at the ocean.

Kate notices something about the water, too. Something that's practically got her hypnotized. "Beautiful," she whispers, like whatever it is, it's a secret between her and herself.

Enough nature worship, though. We've got work to

do. "Think sea monster," I say and scan the shore looking for just the right spot to fish. High tide is just starting to drop, which is good because when the tide is lively, the fish are, too.

"Well?" asks Kate.

"I'm looking for a sandbar," I mumble, gazing beyond the surf for light patches. "If that sea monster is anywhere, it'll be out there near one, having lunch."

"What makes you so sure?"

"Everyone knows that where there's a sandbar, there are fish, especially in the drop-off behind it. A lot of natural bait collects there—stuff like crabs and eels," I tell her. "Bait gets swept up by the tide and winds up trapped in the drop-off. The sandbar turns into a salad bar for fish."

Kate thinks about my explanation, looking for holes I'm sure, but comes up empty. "So you think the fish that are eating at the sandbar will end up being bait for sea monsters?"

"You learn fast," I say.

We both continue to scan the horizon. "There." I point to a long, slim stretch of light-blue water off to our left, about 200 yards out. It's a sandbar all right, one so shallow that waves are breaking over it. "Let's go."

We head down to the shore and drop the equipment on the sand.

"I'm no fishing expert," Kate says, "but I don't need

to be one to know that you can't cast out that far."

"Watch and learn," I say. I poke the two sand spikes deep into the ground, side by side. Then I insert the rods into the holders so they're pointing upright and leaning toward the water just slightly. These aren't the rods Gabe and I use for surfcasting; they're the ones we use for trolling at sea. They're longer and stronger, with 20-pound line and an enormous tuna hook on one of them.

"Why two rods?" asks Kate.

"Patience, patience . . . " I empty the backpack and lay things out: an unassembled kite and the foil-wrapped bait that I took from the refrigerator.

"Now I'm totally confused. You're planning to catch a sea monster with two fishing rods, a balloon, and a kite?"

"Bingo." Kite fishing is really popular in Florida, according to that outdoor sportsman's show Gabe and I watch on cable every week. I'm going to make my own rig. The guy on TV showed us how.

First I put the kite together, tie the balloon to its center for extra lift, and attach it to the line on the hookless rod. Right away, I can feel the wind pulling on it, wanting to take it to Portugal, so I hand it to Kate and tell her, "Don't let go."

Then I bait the hook on the other rod. I pick up the package wrapped in tinfoil and pull out what's inside—

one of the small steaks Mom bought for a barbecue last week that didn't happen because there was no propane left in the grill. It's nice and juicy, downright lip-smackin' . . . to a sea monster, anyway. That is, if sea monsters *have* lips.

Kate scrunches up her face. "Gross."

"Maybe to you. But to a sea monster it'll seem like dessert." I stick the steak onto the hook. Then I pull out the lines from both rods a bit and connect them with a release clip, which looks a little like a metal clothespin.

"How do you know that a steak is going to attract a sea monster?"

"He evolved from a salamander, I'm pretty sure. Salamanders are carnivores. They eat slugs and stuff," I tell Kate as I adjust the two lines so that they run side-by-side through the clip.

"So what? Chihuahuas are carnivores. Doesn't mean they evolved from salamanders."

Always the skeptic. "Yeah, but Chihuahuas don't have tiny heads and legs and big eyes."

"Sure they do."

I think for a second. "OK, maybe they do, but they don't split their time between land and water."

"Ducks split their time between land and water. Doesn't mean they evolved from salamanders, either."

I think for a minute. "Yeah, but ducks are birds, not 'half fish, half lizard,' the way Sidelinger described Old

Orchard. The way salamanders look. Plus, one kind— the giant salamander—is the biggest of all living amphibians. Breathes through its skin. Believe me, there's a connection."

"Who told you all this?"

"I learned it in the library," I answer, feeling pretty proud of myself.

Kate still has questions; I can tell by her expression. But she doesn't say a thing. She just stands there, staring out to sea, holding the kite.

I pull the camera from the backpack, the only remaining item except for a few old candy wrappers. I put the camera on top of the tackle box, away from the sand. Then I check the equipment one last time. One rod has the bait, the other has the kite, both lines are connected, and there's a steady offshore wind. Perfect.

"Let 'er rip!" I shout.

Kate releases the kite. It sails up and out toward the sun, as if a motor was hooked to it instead of a balloon. As the kite angles north, the fishing line drops south. When the kite's about as high as it can go, and the bait is dangling just above the water's surface, just beyond the sandbar, I lock both reels. Then we take the rods out of the sand spikes so that we can feel the tug. And wait.

"Do we reel in both lines when we get a bite?" Kate asks after a few minutes.

"No. Only the fishing line. It'll snap from the kite

line when something pulls on it."

Kate is impressed. "Justin, you are an amazing fisherman. No wonder you won all those trophies."

I nod, as if she's telling me something I don't already know, and watch the bait bob in and out of the water, tempting the lunch crowd. "Hey, what are we going to name our sea monster?" I ask.

"Well, Sidelinger named his after the beach he found her on."

"So we call ours 'Scrub'?" I suggest.

Kate screws up her face the same way she did when she laid eyes on the bait. "I don't like that." Then she says, "This is Rose's Island, so how about 'Rosie'?"

"No sea monster of mine is going to be a girl."

"Old Orchard was a girl, remember?"

She's right. "I guess, but does ours have to have such a girlie name?"

"Don't be such a guy."

Right again. "OK, Rosie is fine."

"Something else, Justin," Kate says. She sounds like she's got bad news.

"What?"

"Old Orchard couldn't have been a salamander—or any kind of amphibian."

"Why not?" I'm hurt. After all my research, Kate's going to try to ruin things.

"Old Orchard must have been a mammal."

"How do you know that?" I ask.

"You said she had babies inside her. If she had been an amphibian, she'd have had eggs."

"Maybe she was a mutant salamander," I suggest. I'm not about to give up on my theory. Not after all the research I did on salamanders. "Or maybe amphibians haven't always laid eggs." I realize that I'm on shaky ground here. Even *I* know that much science. "Anyway, even if Old Orchard was a mammal, she could still be a carnivore." I say.

Kate just shakes her head.

I check my watch. It's almost three o'clock. We stand there for about 15 more minutes watching the kite swirl, the bait bob, and calling out to Rosie to come and get it.

After about a half hour without a bite, though, we get a little tired. We put the rods back into the sand spikes so we can sprawl out.

"This isn't looking good," Kate mutters.

"Takes time," I assure her.

"How do you know? You've never fished for a sea monster before."

"Trust me." And she does, for another hour. In that time, I scan the water, looking for any unusual activity, but all I see are the usual seagulls and swimmers and sailboats. No sea monster, that's for sure.

Another hour passes. "We're wasting our time," Kate whispers.

"No, we're not. I think steak may've been the wrong choice. Should've used live bait."

"Yeah, like a 6-foot earthworm!" says Kate. I can tell by her tone that she's ready to go home. And I guess I am, too. The tide is low now, so the water around the sandbar is really shallow, probably too shallow for any sea monster. I reel in the lines.

"Let's go." We pack up the equipment and head toward the boardwalk. I'm feeling a little disappointed, but not done in. I think about Ted, how it took him five years to catch that 400-pound swordfish hanging on his wall.

The way I figure it, I've got the rest of the summer to figure out how to catch Rosie. And figuring out how to do it doesn't bother me. In fact, it's fun. It's like a puzzle. And it sure beats thinking about my family.

# Chapter Six

# The Setback

**Wednesday morning, August 16th**

"I don't know."

"Yes, you do."

"I don't." I hate it when Leslie thinks she knows me better than I know myself. We're sitting here trying to get through the rest of *Bigfoot: Fact or Fiction*. She asked me to summarize what we've already read so it will make more sense. Things aren't going well.

"You do. You told me just the other day how many documented sightings there have been."

I look her straight in the eye. "I don't know."

She stares right back. "You don't care."

Silence.

Leslie is absolutely right. I don't care about reading. Why should I? It's never done anything but keep me up nights. Mom says that people who don't read, don't learn. But she's wrong. I know lots of people who don't read, and they learn plenty by just living life.

Leslie takes a deep breath. "As we learned the last

time, there have been over 1,000 sightings, mostly in the Pacific Northwest and Canada. People have used photographs, footprints, and their own stories to convince others that Bigfoot really exists. But not everyone believes them." She stops and glances at me. "Are you listening?"

"Yes," I lie. Actually, I'm too busy doodling a rabbit in my reader's journal to listen.

"No, you're not." She slides the book under my nose. "Please read this page," she says, sounding like that lady who tested me and a bunch of other kids last year. No one ever told us how bad we did on those tests. But we knew.

My eyes slide over the first sentence: "In 1970, Dr. John Napier examined a trail of 1,089 successive, 17-inch footprints that were discovered in the snow near Bossburg, Washington."

Easy enough, I think. But when I try to say it, it comes out all wrong, especially when I hit "successive." I slam the book shut and push it aside. "I can't."

Leslie picks it up, and in a gentler voice asks, "How about if I read to you?"

I say nothing. Instead, I drop my head onto my folded arms.

"OK," she continues. "Maybe we should save old Bigfoot for another day." She pushes the book aside this time. "What's bothering you?"

"Can't read," I answer, without lifting my head.

"Believe me, you can read. If anyone should know, it's me, your wise old reading teacher."

I turn toward her, so that my ear is resting on my elbow, and smile.

"Actually, I'm seeing improvement with each session. Here, let me show you." Leslie flips a few pages back in her writing pad and explains all the good things I've started doing, like predicting, asking questions, and using whole sentences to help me figure out big words.

"Maybe I *can* read," I say reluctantly.

"Of course you can read, Justin. And you're going to be an even better reader by the time I'm done with you." She grabs the Bigfoot book. "So do you want to finish this?"

I give it some thought. She's convinced me that I can read, but I don't *want* to. Not right now, anyway. "Not really."

"Why? You were totally into it on Monday."

"I'm not sure," I answer.

"Did something happen at home?"

Remember how I said that sometimes Leslie can see inside my head? Well, it seems she just put on her x-ray glasses.

"Maybe."

"What?" she asks. Nothing more, and now I've got to fill the air.

"Gabe."

"What about Gabe?"

"He's a jerk."

She taps her chin. "That's interesting. I've heard you call him an awesome storyteller, surfcaster, and Frisbee® player, but never a jerk. Did something happen?"

I don't want to discuss it, but keeping it inside would take way too much work. "I borrowed his fishing equipment without asking and he had a fit."

"Why?"

"I dunno. Maybe he was having a bad day."

"No, why did you borrow his equipment without asking?"

"Because I wanted to use it, and he would've said no." How's that for telling her the truth?

"Justin, you're old enough to know that you shouldn't use other people's things without getting permission."

Whatever. "I've used his equipment a million times before. There was no way I was going to break it or lose it or anything."

"So then why didn't you ask him first?" Leslie asks.

Do I tell her the whole truth? That I needed his equipment for sea-monster fishing? I take a deep breath. "Can you keep a secret?"

"Sure."

"Kate and I needed it to catch our own Old

Orchard. I was afraid that if I told Gabe, he would've laughed me off the island."

"What?" Looks like Leslie could use a stronger x-ray eyeglass prescription because she clearly didn't see that answer coming.

"Didn't catch anything, though . . . except grief from Gabe. I thought I put everything back exactly where I found it, but he spotted a rod out of place. Lucky for me he didn't notice anything funny about the video camera."

"Video camera?"

"Yeah. See, Kate and I aren't planning to catch and keep our sea monster, the way Sidelinger did. We want to catch and film it, the way Roger Patterson did with Bigfoot. Then we'll set it free."

"I see," says Leslie, sounding like the special-ed lady again and staring at me like I've got problems. Big ones.

"Anyway, Gabe doesn't miss a thing when it comes to his stuff. Protects it like it's made out of gold or something. I should've been more careful about putting everything back."

"Or maybe you shouldn't have taken it in the first place," said Leslie. "How would you like it if Gabe went into your room and borrowed your skateboard without asking?"

"Whose side are you on?" I snap.

"Nobody's. I'm just saying that taking other people's

stuff isn't the smartest thing to do."

Grown-ups. They're *all* a bunch of jerks. "Gabe wouldn't take my skateboard. He broke his elbow on one when he was 12, and he says he'll never ride again."

"That's not the point."

It's not the point, for sure. The point is that I'm tired of Gabe always talking, never listening. Being so stuck on himself. Treating life like one big joke. That is, of course, until I do something that he doesn't find amusing. Like borrowing his fishing equipment. Complaining about the twins. And not laughing when I'm supposed to.

I drop my head back onto my folded arms.

Leslie sighs loudly. "I'm sorry if it felt like I was taking sides, Justin. It sounds like you and Gabe are going through a rough patch. You'll work it out."

"No," I say into my arms. Then I raise my head. Suddenly, things seem clearer than they have in a long time. Our eyes lock. "I hate him. Will forever. It's that simple."

Leslie frowns and looks away. It seems like we're going down a road that she doesn't want to be on. Can't say I blame her, either. After all, she's my reading teacher, not my shrink.

But I *do* hate him.

Leslie changes the subject. "Tell me more about what you were doing with his equipment in the first place. Trying to catch your own Old Orchard, you said?"

Finally, a subject that deserves airtime. "Yep, but don't tell anyone."

"You know, Justin, people don't generally catch sea monsters by fishing for them. They spot them when they least expect it."

Leslie's nice, but she's way too sensible. She should work on that. "I know, but maybe that's because no one's ever tried. I mean, folks hunt Bigfoot all the time. Why not Rosie?"

"Who?"

"Rosie. That's her name."

"Whose?"

I'm starting to wonder who's tutoring who here. "The sea monster we're going to catch!"

"OK, let me get this straight," says Leslie. " You took Gabe's equipment out to the beach to try to catch a sea monster."

"Right." I tell Leslie everything. That Kate and I met at Scrub Point at two o'clock, and I wasn't even late. That the tide was just right for fishing, but the time of day wasn't. That we located a sandbar. That we used a kite and a balloon to get the raw steak out past it. And that although we had the camera ready, we didn't use it because we didn't even get a nibble. Not yet, anyway.

"Why did you use steak for bait?"

"Well, I did a little research at the library, see." I roll

my eyes up to get a look at Leslie's reaction. It's just what I expect: a combination of excitement and shock that I would do such a thing. "And I discovered that, most likely, Rosie evolved from a salamander." I've decided not to throw in Kate's arguments for Rosie being a mammal. Kate could be wrong, after all. *She* didn't do the research.

"What made you decide that?"

"It was easy. If you think about the description of Old Orchard that we read, you'll see that sea monsters and salamanders have a lot in common."

"Really. Like what?"

I tell Leslie all the connections I'd found—that they're carnivores with tiny heads and legs and big eyes. That they're nature's answer to surf-and-turf because they divide their time between water and land. That they have lungs, but breathe through their skin, too.

"Sidelinger didn't say anything about Old Orchard breathing through its skin."

OK, maybe I slipped that in because it sounds neat. "But he did say everything else."

"How do their sizes compare?"

"The giant salamander is the largest amphibian on Earth," I say, talking more like the book than myself.

"How do their sizes compare?"

She's tough. "Salamanders are a little smaller," I admit.

"How much smaller?"

I do the math. "About 145 feet."

"Justin, I hate to disappoint you, but I don't think Old Orchard evolved from a salamander."

"What makes you so sure?" I know what's coming.

"What the scientists said back in 1905. Old Orchard was a mammal; salamanders aren't. Don't forget the title of Sidelinger's pamphlet—*The Real Sea Serpent: The Most Marvelous Mammal in Creation.*"

Oh, yeah. A detail I had missed when reading. Kate was right—again.

Now Leslie motions me down to the computer station and logs us onto the cryptozoology site. We search for "Old Orchard" and skim the Web page again. "See, Justin," Leslie says, pointing out parts of the article. "She had the respiratory, skeletal, and reproductive systems of a mammal. If Old Orchard wasn't a blue whale, she was most likely the ugly cousin of one."

I push back from the monitor. "What do scientists know?"

"A lot."

I'm fed up, and Leslie must sense it because she puts a hand on my shoulder.

"So do you think Old Orchard was just some kind of freaky-looking whale?" I ask.

"Well, I don't know. I'd need to do more research."

"I already did research," I say, feeling like it's a lost cause.

"Doing research isn't like watching a TV show. You don't finish it in a half hour and move on. You keep at it until you've found satisfying answers."

I let that soak in.

"Tell you what," Leslie continues, "I'm going to Boston next Saturday for a teachers' workshop. While I'm there, I'll stop by the public library to see if I can find more information about Old Orchard. But only on one condition."

"What?"

"You go back to our library and do the same. Then we'll compare notes."

How did I wind up in this position? Held hostage by my tutor? I feel like I'm being brainwashed, like she's trying to turn me into something I'm not. Some kind of brainy dork. I can see the nightmares coming. Instead of being forced to read to the kids in my class, I'll be forced to help them with book reports and science projects. Join the computer club. Wind up class president. My life is over. But what can I do? I'm a hostage.

"Deal," I answer.

"Good." Leslie grabs the Bigfoot book because, once again, she's bamboozled me into a good mood. And when I'm in a good mood, I read.

So I dive in, but my mind isn't entirely on the book. It's on Rosie. As far as I'm concerned, a sea monster's a sea monster. It just so happens that maybe this one evolved from a whale, not a salamander. Whether you're a human being or a sea monster or a Chihuahua, you had to have evolved from something, come from somewhere, right? So maybe I just need to change my strategy. Maybe I need to think big. Maybe I need to move on.

# Chapter Seven

# The Surprise

*Saturday morning, August 19th*

For most kids, Saturday is the best day of the week because they get to do whatever they feel like, with no parent conferences or piano lessons to get in the way. But, in case it hasn't sunk in, I'm not like most kids.

On Saturdays—*every* Saturday—we visit my grandfather. He lives about a half hour south of Rose's Island in an apartment complex called Evergreen Estates. He's actually Mom's grandfather, which makes him my great-grandfather. So he's really old, like 80, and needs help doing normal things like taking a bath. I guess that's why they call his complex "assisted living."

"Let's go, Champ," Gabe shouts from the bottom of the stairs. "Champ." "Sport." What is this, a football game? Why can't he just call me what Mom did eleven years ago? Justin. I feel like shouting back, "I'll be right there, Coach," but I bite my tongue and ignore him instead.

A little history about my great-grandfather: Mom's parents got divorced, too, when she was a kid. I'm not sure why exactly. They just did. And they totally abandoned Mom and her sister, my Aunt Louise—the one who brought Mom the mug from Ireland. So their grandparents jumped in and raised the two of them.

I know it's complicated, but I just wanted to make it clear that walking out on kids is a tradition my family's had for generations. Like Thanksgiving.

Mom's grandmother, my great-grandmother, the wife of the guy we're visiting today, was the best. I'd spend hours making things with her in the kitchen—cookies, candles, and stained-glass window ornaments that weren't really made out of glass but colorful plastic chips that we'd put into compartments of frames shaped like angels and frogs and flowers and stuff, and then bake in the oven at 375 degrees for ten minutes.

When they cooled, we'd hang them on the window on little suction cups. And then we'd light our candles and eat our cookies and talk. I remember the sun coming through the window and hitting our stained-glass ornaments, splashing the colors all over us. She liked the angels most.

And then she got cancer and died. At first I was mad at her for doing that. Maybe not mad, but disappointed in her for leaving me like my father did. Now I just feel sad because she couldn't do much about it. It's taken me five years to figure that out. That sometimes people don't *choose* to leave.

I hear footsteps at the bottom of the stairs, and then Mom. "Justin, now!" She's not happy. But still I take my time tying my shoes, making the knots perfect. Tight so they don't come undone. Just the way she likes them.

Back to Grandma. When she died, a big part of Grandpa did, too. He started going to bed early and getting up late. Eating nothing but TV dinners, right where you're supposed to eat them: in front of the TV. Crying sometimes, which was weird because I was so used to seeing him laugh. Laugh so hard the sofa would shake.

Then his health took a nosedive. He started having trouble walking and breathing, so bad that even medicines didn't help. Then right after a party to celebrate my first fishing derby victory, Grandpa had a little heart attack. That's when Mom and Aunt Louise decided that living on his own was a bad idea. So they sold his house and moved him to Evergreen.

At first he wasn't happy. But now he is. I think it's because the nurses don't treat him like he's made out of glass. In fact, they're always telling him how handsome and charming he is, a real catch for any woman at Evergreen. And believe me, there are plenty of women there. There's gotta be at least ten for every man. But Grandpa would never get married again. Because even though Grandma's dead, she's still there for him. At least, that's what I think.

My bedroom door flies open, and guess who's behind it? Mom—her eyes flashing. "Justin, get in the car this instant."

"OK, OK. I was just tying my shoes." I follow her orders and walk down the stairs and outside into the clear blue day. It's perfect weather for hunting sea monsters. That won't happen, though, until I figure out a new strategy.

Gabe's already behind the wheel of the car. Mom climbs in next to him with the grace of a rhinoceros. All belly.

I hop into the big back seat, which is the best thing about this car. I'm the smallest person, yet I always get the biggest seat. When I was little, I used to line my action figures up on the window ledge. Then I'd pretend to be an intergalactic sorcerer and knock them off, one by one.

Not anymore, though. I'm too old for that. Now instead of pretending I'm a sorcerer, I pretend I'm invisible.

"Hey, sport, what did you think of that movie last night?

Clearly my invisibility shield isn't working. "It was all right."

"I thought the special effects were pretty good, considering that they didn't have computer graphics back in the '70s."

Whatever. Looks like he's not mad at me anymore, which is a shame because, if he were, I wouldn't have to decide whether to talk to him. He never stays mad for long. "Had a big budget. Big budget, big effects," I answer.

"You're right." Gabe looks at me in the rearview mirror, giving me a 60-watt smile, as if we've just had some incredibly meaningful conversation.

I look away. We're off the island now, riding down River Street toward the highway that takes us to Grandpa's. We pass Ted's boat club, Brenda's restaurant, and the health club Mom went to before the twins made that impossible.

"I baked Grandpa some cookies," she says, holding up a plate covered in plastic wrap. "Want one?"

I nod, and she lifts the edge of the wrap, turns slightly, and holds the plate out to me. My crack about always feeding us take-out must've really hit home.

"How many hermits does it take to screw in a light-bulb?" Gabe asks.

Here we go—the jokester's at it again. Mom mulls his question over. I don't.

"Give up?"

"Yes!" I shout.

"None. They'd rather sit in the dark," he says.

No one laughs.

"Get it?" Gabe asks. "Hermits don't like being

around people, so they would probably like to sit in the dark. Because then nobody would see them."

Give it up. If you have to explain a joke, you shouldn't have told it in the first place.

Gabe pulls onto the highway, and we start down it like we always do. One long stretch until Exit 53. But for some reason, today Gabe pulls off at Exit 48.

"Gabe, what are you doing?" asks Mom.

"We need gas."

Mom checks the dashboard. "No, we don't. We've got three-quarters of a tank."

"Better safe than sorry," he says.

Mom's not convinced. "What are you talking about?"

"Oh, nothing," he answers.

I'm silent. He's definitely up to something, but I'm not about to give him the satisfaction of trying to figure it out. We make a couple more turns and wind up in the parking lot of Moody's, the place where Mom and Gabe had their wedding reception.

"Oh, please," says Mom, like suddenly she knows exactly what he's doing. She's not happy. I, on the other hand, don't have a clue.

We get out of the car and head for the entrance. On the way, Mom pleads, "Please don't do this to me," like Gabe's forcing her into the barbershop for a crew cut.

What is going on?

Gabe holds open the door for us and we go in—first Mom, then me, then Gabe. My eyes take a second to adjust to the dark, and then everything becomes clear. I see a wall of faces, then hear one big, ear-splitting shout of "Surprise!"

I jump a mile and then take a step back, into the light, while my heart adjusts to the shock. Everyone's here: Aunt Louise, Brenda, Ted, George, Grandpa in his wheelchair, and a ton of others whose names I can't remember. I look over their heads and see that the room is decorated with streamers and balloons. I spot waiters with food trays. And—next to a table loaded down with presents—Kate. What a relief.

The crowd rushes us like we're some hot new rock band. Everyone starts kissing Mom and asking how she's feeling. She makes a few comments about being stunned, about the possibility of going into labor at this very moment. Everyone thinks that's a riot.

Gabe gets little pecks from the women and hand-shakes from the men. And what do I get? Pats on the head, as usual, like a dog. Some lady Mom used to work with crouches down and gives me a big, goofy grin. "It must be so exciting to be the future brother of twins," she says.

Yeah, I think, about as exciting as yard work. But I nod because that's the polite thing to do and tell her I have to go to the bathroom even though I don't.

Breaking away isn't easy because of all the bodies, but I manage, giving Grandpa a quick kiss along the way. I make a beeline for Kate.

"Surprise," she says with a yawn. Seems she doesn't want to be here, either.

"Whose idea was this?"

"Gabe and my mom's. Who else would think of it?"

I suppose it was a nice thing to do, but why didn't they let me in on the secret? Kate and I stand there trying to decide whether to be good kids who circulate among the guests, or bad kids who grab some food and leave.

"I'm starving," says Kate.

I like her style.

We belly up to the food table. The centerpiece is somebody's strange idea of cuteness: Two baby dolls stuck in a basket with Easter grass and fake daisies. I grab a paper plate and pile on little quiches, deviled eggs, spinach squares, chicken fingers, and brownies. Kate does the same. Then we head out the back door to avoid the fuss.

It's only eleven o'clock and already another scorcher. So we plop down in a shady spot next to the dumpster to eat. I start with the brownies.

We just sit there without talking, but that's OK. Kate and I do that all the time—don't talk but still hear each other. And what I'm hearing now isn't good.

"You all right, Kate?"

"I was supposed to be with my dad today, but Mom made me come here instead."

"We're not that far from Boston. Maybe she could drive you down after the party. Or we could," I tell her through a mouthful of spinach squares.

"No. Dad decided to take off for the weekend when he found out that I couldn't come at my usual time." She shoves her plate to one side with half the food still on it.

"You going to eat that?"

She slides it over to me. "Do you realize how bad that stuff is for you?"

"Then why did you take it in the first place?"

She can't answer. She's too caught up thinking about

her father. I can tell. So I try to come up with something that will make her feel better. "It's only one weekend, Kate."

She shakes her head. "This is the second time this summer he's left town without me."

"Well, he's got stuff he wants to do."

"And on Sundays, he's been bringing me home earlier and earlier. Used to be seven at night. Now it's more like three in the afternoon. He's sick of me."

We get all quiet again, listen to laughs coming from inside the hall, and think about our fathers. After a while, Kate lifts her head from her bent knees. "In some ways you're lucky. You never have to worry about your dad ditching you, because he already did, a long time ago."

"That's right. And now I'm stuck with a stepfather who's in it for the long haul. He's not going anywhere, that's for sure. Unfortunately."

"Gabe's not so bad."

"He's a jerk. Trust me."

"Do you ever think about your real dad?"

"How can you think about someone you can't even remember?"

And I can't, hardly. I have one fuzzy memory of sitting on his lap, blowing bubbles. I remember his mustache. I remember his blue tank top. I remember the little bubble wand in his big hand—him dipping it into the purple plastic bottle, pulling it out, and blowing.

I remember the bubbles floating against the sky—a sky with no clouds—catching the sunlight, and then bursting. Gone. Dad was about as permanent as one of those bubbles.

"No, I don't think about him," I say.

"Ever?" she asks, like she doesn't believe me.

"Ever. All I know is he lives in Brooklyn, New York. That's what's printed on his support checks anyway." This conversation is weighing down on me like a loaded lobster trap.

Suddenly, I get an urge I can't fight. I stand up and start singing like a wild man, stomping around the dumpster, banging on it with an old stewed-tomato can. "Fathers, fathers, I hate fathers!"

I lean toward the door with hopes that someone will hear me, especially Gabe. "Fathers, fathers, I hate fathers!" I sing out from the deepest part of me.

Kate grabs my shirt and pulls me down. "Have you lost your mind?"

I fall in a heap on the ground, laughing. "That felt good! You should try it."

"You're crazy."

I look at her googly-eyed, stick my thumbs in my armpits, and start doing my best chicken call. And, finally, Kate starts laughing, too.

"Let's talk about something else," I suggest.

"Like what?"

"Sea monsters."

"What about them?"

I tell Kate about my talk with Leslie. About how she—Kate—was right. Old Orchard was a mammal, probably a relative of a whale, but not a whale. She was definitely a sea monster. Sort of.

"What makes you so sure there's another one out there, almost 100 years later?" she asks, eating a deviled egg, which is suddenly good for you, I guess.

"There's more than one tuna in the ocean, isn't there? More than one bass? More than one cod? More than one pollock, mackerel, haddock—"

"OK, OK. I get your point."

"Rosie's out there, I know. She just hasn't found us yet. But she will."

"Justin," Kate says, searching for a kind way to tell me something I don't want to hear. "Be reasonable."

No time for reason, because I just had an idea. A brilliant one. "Can you meet me at Harrison's dock on Monday?" I ask her.

"Sure, what time?"

"Four."

"Yep. I have science camp until three, so I'll head over after that."

"No, four in the *morning*."

# Chapter Eight

# The Quest, Part Two

*Monday morning, August 21st*

Sleep is a weird thing. I mean, most nights I just flop into bed, fall asleep in no time, and don't come to until dawn. Some nights I get to sleep just as fast, but then one of those reading nightmares hits, and I wind up staring at the ceiling for hours, wide awake, thinking I'm the dumbest thing on Earth.

And some nights I just don't fall asleep at all because I'm too caught up in what's going to happen the next day. Like Christmas, for example. Well, last night was one of those nights. I crawled into bed at about ten o'clock, as usual, flipped through the new skateboard catalog, and turned out the light when Mom noticed that it was still on at eleven.

I've been lying here for hours, in the dark, eye to eye with Rosie. Kate and I are going to catch her today. It's three in the morning now; by 7:30, I figure, we'll be heroes, just like Sidelinger and Patterson. I know it.

See, I did a little research at the library yesterday afternoon and got all my facts straight. Revised my plan. And last night, after dinner, I gathered the equipment while Mom and Gabe wrote thank-you notes for the baby gifts. It's waiting for me downstairs in the garage. All I have to do is hop on my bike and go.

Escaping without waking anyone up won't be easy, though. When the babies make it hard for Mom to sleep, she gets up and wanders around.

I push the covers off and sit up. No need to get dressed because I already am. I'm wearing my jeans and my lucky T-shirt. I grab my sneakers and jacket because it can get cold where I'm going, even in August. Then I tiptoe out my bedroom door—which I left open a crack so I wouldn't have to worry about knob noise.

Gabe and Mom's bedroom is at the other end of the hall, thank goodness, so I don't have to deal with sneaking by their door or anything. I just take a quick left down the staircase, doing my best to avoid the creaky treads, which I found last night by doing a little dance on every one of them.

The front door is at the bottom of the staircase, but I don't use it because it's noisy. Instead, I head for the kitchen, grab a stale doughnut from a box sitting on the counter, and slip out the back.

The damp, dark night wraps around me like the chocolate coating on my doughnut, so I put on my jacket and then my sneakers. The garage is separate from the house, across the yard at the end of the driveway. It was much easier to see last night because of the light from the kitchen window. I can sort of make out the white frame, so I head that way. As I get closer and my eyes fine-tune themselves to the moonlight, the garage and everything around it becomes easier to see.

I edge along the side wall, the one facing the house, in case Mom gets up and peeks outside. Then I duck into the garage through the main door, which I left open last night. I strap on my backpack, slip the three coils of rope over one shoulder, and tuck the video camera in a milk crate fastened behind the bike seat. The garden rakes are already tied to the handlebars. Everything's set.

I wheel the bike as quietly as possible to the end of the driveway and hop on. I'm off. Free. I pedal fast, faster than a fugitive on the run, because it stops me from thinking too much about what I'm about to do. Stops me from changing my mind. I am taking a big risk, after all. If Gabe catches me this time, I'm grounded for life.

I ride down my road, to the main street, and onto the small bridge that links the island to the mainland. I'm not usually out at this time of day, of course, so it's strange to see the water glittering in the moonlight. The stars filling the sky. A glow on the horizon. It's kind of pretty. Then I remember reports of coyotes from the wildlife refuge stalking the streets at night looking for food. I pump faster.

No one's out. No one. I sail right down the middle of River Street without worrying about cars or coyotes turning me into roadkill. I make it to the entrance of Harrison's in record time. In fact, I beat Kate!

This part of town is brighter than my neighborhood because of the streetlights, but it's still too dark to see where I'm going. So I take the flashlight out of the backpack, flick it on, and make my way down to the docks. I can make out the boat shapes in the water, just barely. They look like big white ironing boards, all in a row.

I peel the backpack from my shoulders, drop it on the wooden walkway, and start looking around for slip seven, Gabe's slip. Then I hear a bike rattle, followed by a tiny voice. "Justin? Is that you?"

"Yeah, it's me," I answer, right out loud.

"Shhhh . . ." Kate says, coming closer. Close enough for me to make out her shape.

"Nobody's out here, believe me."

"Nobody in their right mind, that is," she says crossly. "So it makes perfect sense we're here, I guess."

She's already giving me a headache. "Don't get started. After all, today's the day we catch us a sea monster. Smile!"

"You drag me out of bed at three in the morning, and you expect me to smile?"

She does have a point. "OK, you don't have to smile. You just have to do whatever I say."

"Depends on what you say."

"Help me carry this stuff over to the boat," I tell her, handing her the rope and pointing my chin toward the walkway leading to Gabe's fishing boat.

"I'm calling the police." Kate turns to leave.

I grab her arm. "Wait. I'm telling you, I can do this. I've driven this boat a million times before. I can do this."

Kate looks at me the way Mrs. Heaney did when I suggested comic books for reading group. "You've had some crazy ideas before, but this one takes the prize. Justin, it's pitch black out."

"I checked the marine report. Sunrise is in a half hour. Trust me. I know what I'm doing." Truth of the matter, though, is I don't completely know what I'm doing. Sure, I've driven the boat before, but never alone, never without Gabe sitting next to me, telling me when to speed up, when to slow down, when to turn, and in what direction. But I can't tell Kate that. Then I'd really be on my own.

"I do trust you," Kate says. "But you're overlooking one tiny fact: it's against the law. You don't have a boat license."

OK, she's got me on that one. So I do what any promising young cryptozoologist would do—ignore her. "Help me with this stuff."

Kate takes the rope and picks up the backpack. "I'll help you load the boat, but you're on your own from there."

Convincing her is going to be a bigger job than I thought. "There's no way this plan can fail," I say, grabbing the rakes, video camera, and tackle box. "I went to the library yesterday and did a little research on whales." I carefully place the camera on a starboard seat and hop on board. This boat is tiny compared to Ted's, only 16 feet. No flybridge. No staterooms. No entertainment center. Gabe named it "The Beast," which is like naming a goldfish "Jaws."

Kate doesn't follow. She stands on the dock, her arms folded. "Why whales?"

"I decided you were right. Old Orchard wasn't related to any salamander. If she was related to anything, it was a blue whale, biggest animal on Earth."

"So," says Kate, like she's late for an appointment.

"So here's my theory: Old Orchard didn't evolve from a whale. Whales evolved from Old Orchard. Get it? She was a freak of nature, stuck in time, just like Bigfoot. A lot of scientists think he's stuck in prehistoric time."

"I'm calling the police and telling them to bring a straitjacket."

She starts walking away, but I just keep on talking. Facts—that's what I need here. Nothing else will get to Kate. She loves facts. "Whales have been around for about 60 million years. They crept out of the sea like most mammals, but for some reason they went back in, while the others stayed on the beach. No one's sure why."

Kate stops. It's working.

"Old Orchard was probably an ancestor of the ba-ba-baleen whale." I stumble on the word, but finally get it. "She didn't have any teeth."

"What does not having teeth have to do with anything?" Kate asks.

She's caving in!

"Good question." I start spitting out what I learned at the library—as much as I can remember. "Scientists think that once all whales had teeth. But as time went by, some of them, the ancestors of the baleens, changed. They developed things that are like filters—"

Kate turns. "OK, stop. I hear enough of this kind of talk at science camp. And speaking of which, I can't go with you. I have to be there at nine."

"I have tutoring at nine. That's almost five hours away, plenty of time to hook Rosie, snap a picture, and get ourselves back in bed as if nothing happened."

A long silence. Even in the half-light I can see that Kate is thinking. That's a good sign.

"Oh, all right," she says. "If I don't go, who'll keep you out of trouble? More trouble than you're already going to be in, I mean." She boards the boat and plops down in one of the seats. "And just how are you planning to hook her this time?"

"We'll troll with these." I hold up one of the garden rakes. "See, I'm gonna tie this end to the back of the boat," I say, pointing to the hole at the end of the rake handle. I turn the rake around. "Then I'm gonna tie fishing line to each of the prongs. I'll bait the lines with these." I open the tackle box and pull out a lure that looks like a sardine. "If we throw enough of 'em out, and pull 'em along at the right speed, it'll look like a whole school of small fish. Rosie's breakfast. And then we've got her. Get it?"

"I get it. What's the right speed?"

"About 15 miles an hour. That's how fast blue whales are supposed to swim."

"Won't the engine noise scare her?"

"Not if we let the rakes get far enough from the boat. That's why I brought long ropes."

Kate still seems to have her doubts, but at least she doesn't share them. Instead she asks, "OK, what's next?" Looks like she's really in.

I hand her a spool of 20-pound line. "Start attaching 3-foot lengths of this to each of the rake's prongs. Then tie lures to the ends. Make sure you knot 'em good and tight."

We start in. It's still too dark to sail, but it's bright enough to work because of the light that's peeking up over the horizon. "Sun'll be up soon," I say.

We work away like two old ladies in a quilting circle—measuring, cutting, fastening, measuring, cutting, fastening. It's kind of brainless, so we also watch the sky change over the water. First we see pink, a slash of it just above the horizon. Within minutes, the slash starts morphing into something fuzzier. Swirls of color like I've never seen before. Remember how I said the ocean has all kinds of blues? Well, I see now—right at this very moment—that the sky has all kinds of reds: orange ones and yellow ones and pink ones and even purple ones. And just when I think it can't possibly get more beautiful, it does. The sun starts surfacing, shining, and screaming like it's being born.

Then I come to my senses and notice we've stopped everything else because we're so caught up in the scenery. "Back to work!" I bark.

"Aye, aye, captain," Kate snorts.

When we finish baiting, I tie one end of each rope through the hole on a rake handle. Then I tie the opposite ends of the ropes to the legs of the fishing seats, which are bolted down at the back of the boat. Finally, I check the video camera. It's all juiced up and ready to roll. And so are we. I untie the boat from the dock pilings.

Kate takes the passenger's seat and I, of course, the driver's. I pull the key from my pocket and stick it into the ignition. "Are you ready?"

"Ready!"

I turn the key. The engine roars. In fact, it roars so loud, it's all I can hear. But just as I'm about to throw the boat into drive, I feel a hand on my shoulder . . . and it isn't Kate's.

It's Gabe's.

# Chapter Nine

# The Escape

**Monday morning, August 21st**

"Off!" he shouts over the engine. "Turn it off!"

I twist the key backward. The noise sputters to silence. I turn around. Gabe is looking down at me, still in the gym shorts and T-shirt he wears to bed. The sun's up all the way now, so I can see the anger in his face. Feel the fear in my stomach.

"What exactly do you think you're doing?" he asks, tossing the rope around the pilings so we don't drift off.

I'm not sure what to say. And even if I could think of anything, I don't think it would come out because the fear in my stomach has now climbed up into my throat. So I drop my head and whisper, "I dunno."

"You don't know?" Gabe throws his hands in the air, then bends over and sticks his face into mine. "You *don't know* that you snuck out of the house with my equipment *again*? You *don't know* that you almost took this boat out without an adult? You *don't know* that you could've killed yourselves?"

For the first time he looks at Kate. "And you. I thought you were smarter than this."

Kate avoids his eyes and starts biting her thumbnail because that's what she does when she's nervous. "Sorry."

"Sorry. Is that all you can say?" He just keeps getting madder, as if anything we say is going to be wrong. He looks around the boat and notices the three garden rakes, all baited and waiting to be tossed over the stern. "What are these for?"

Now I really don't know what to say. Am I supposed to tell him the truth? Or keep on lying? Whether I tell the truth or not, I figure, I'll still be in hot water, so I might as well lie. That way Rosie will stay a secret. Just like she ought to be.

"We were going to use them to catch . . ." I can't think of any believable fish.

Gabe's holding one of the rakes now, studying the lines and lures that hang from its prongs. He's starting to look more confused than angry. "Yes?"

"To catch . . . um . . ." My mind's blank.

"A sea monster," Kate blurts out.

I can't believe she told him that. She looks at me as if she's really sorry.

Gabe turns back to me. "Start talking, Justin." His expression tells me that I'd better tell him everything.

"There's a sea monster out there. I know it. And we

were going to catch it by surface trolling. See, I did some research and found out that the monster most likely evolved from a whale. A baleen. See, baleens feed on schools of small fish—"

Gabe holds up his left hand, palm out, like he's trying to stop traffic. "Quiet." Guess he's heard enough. "Pack this stuff up and get in the car. We're going home." Now he's mega-mad. So mad he doesn't even need to talk because everything he's thinking is right there, hanging in the air like gas fumes.

I stuff as much as I can, as fast as I can, into the tackle box and backpack. Kate grabs the rakes. Gabe, the video camera. We step off the boat one at a time and head for

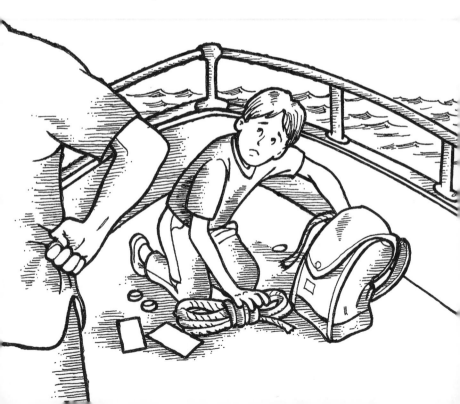

the parking lot, single file. "How did you find us?" I ask, but get no answer.

When we reach the car, Gabe says, "Unlock the bikes and put them in the trunk." We do and he ties the trunk down and gets in the car. Meanwhile, Kate and I throw the equipment and then ourselves into the back seat.

All I can see of Gabe are his eyes in the rearview mirror, looking at me. Looking at me in disgust. Oh, to be invisible.

He starts the car without a word. In fact, he says nothing all the way to Kate's house. He stops in front without even saying good-bye to her, without even turning around. He just sits there, waiting for her to get out.

As Kate pushes the door open, she looks at me with sad eyes, and whispers, "I'll call you." She lifts her bike from the trunk—no help from Gabe. Then she watches as we drive away, just standing there until we're out of view, like she might never see me again. Maybe the situation is worse than I think.

Gabe pulls into our driveway, gets out, and opens the back door for me. "In the house," he snaps.

"What about the equipment?"

"In the house." He must be mad. He never leaves his equipment in the car for fear it might get stolen. But since I've now stolen it twice this week, I guess he's gotten used to the idea.

I march up to the front door and go inside. Mom's in the living room, in her purple bathrobe, a mug of tea in her hand. "What's going on? Where were you?"

I feel Gabe's eyes on me. "Tell her," he says.

"Harrison's."

"Harrison's? What were you doing there?" she asks.

"Tell her."

Man, he sure repeats himself a lot. "Kate and I were going to take the boat out. Do a little fishing."

Mom blinks. "You were going to *what?*"

But before I can answer, Gabe cuts in. "They were going to take the boat out on a joyride, alone. I stopped them just as they were leaving the dock."

"Wasn't a joyride," I mumble, half wanting them to hear, half not wanting them to. Doesn't matter anyway, because Gabe isn't paying attention.

"It was a joyride. Some cockamamie scheme to catch a sea monster."

Mom presses a hand against her middle, as if she's trying to shield the twins from something terrible. "What?"

"It wasn't cockamamie," I tell him.

"You think two 11-year-old kids taking a motorboat out to sea by themselves isn't cockamamie?" he says. "You don't know how to navigate those waters. That channel has one of the strongest pulls on the East Coast. You could've died."

Died. Yeah, right. He's seen me drive that boat. He knows I can navigate those waters better than a lot of guys who've had their licenses for years. He knows. After all, he taught me.

I can't listen to him. So I tell him I'm sorry, even though I'm not, and head out of the room to get a bowl of cereal.

"Stop right there!" he shouts. "Sorry isn't good enough."

"What else do you want me to say?" I ask, still facing the kitchen.

"I'm not sure, but I'm going to give you lots of time to think about it." Gabe comes up behind me, spins me around, and looks into my eyes like he never has before. Like he can't stand the sight of me. "I don't want you leaving this house for the rest of the summer for anything except tutoring. That means no bike, no beach, no Kate, no sea monster. Nothing. Clear?"

The rest of the summer? Is he nuts? That's two whole weeks. I look to Mom to stick up for me, but she doesn't. In fact, she seems pretty upset herself. Who needs her, anyway? Who needs him? "Fine," I holler and run up the stairs to my room, slamming the door behind me as loudly as I can.

I throw myself onto the furry beanbag chair I got for my birthday and think. Think about that question—who needs him? He's not even my father, so what gives him the right to lay down the law? To act that way at all, ever? And that's all it is—an act. A real father would talk to me and listen. Wouldn't treat me like his pal one day, a prisoner the next. Who needs him?

I bury my face in the beanbag chair, thinking about how horrible the rest of the summer is going to be. Stuck in this house for two weeks, then off to school, which is just another form of punishment as far as I'm concerned. I hate my life. I hate Gabe.

I look at the clock and notice the time. Two hours until tutoring. Thinking about Leslie makes me feel better. Maybe she can help me. After all, that's what she was hired to do. Then again, helping me lose my stepfather is probably not in her job description. But there are other things she can do.

I think about our last session, how nice she was, how well she treated me, how great she made me feel about myself, like always. Gabe could learn a thing or two from Leslie.

I think about the deal we struck—me doing research here in town, her doing research when she goes to Boston this Saturday. Wait until I tell her I fulfilled my end of the bargain yesterday! And did it right this time. I got all kinds of information on baleen whales and their connection to sea monsters. Possible connection, that is. She's not going to believe it. Then again, what difference does it make? The hunt for Rosie ended this morning. Evidence or no evidence, that sea monster isn't gonna be headline news anytime soon. Might as well just tell Leslie to forget about Boston.

Then suddenly, an idea hits me like a jet ski slamming into a huge wave. Leslie's trip could be my ticket out of here. Just the excuse I need to leave forever. Find my real dad. Start a whole new life. All Leslie has to do is get me as far as Boston. From there, I can take a train to New York. I know I can because I did it before, when Mom, Aunt Louise, Grandpa, and I went there for Thanksgiving weekend a few years ago. It's easy. A kid's ticket costs $35. I've already saved more than that for my new skateboard. This could work.

The more I think about it, though, the more problems I see—like giving Leslie a good excuse for wanting to go with her. I mean, I can't tell her the truth—that I need her to drive the getaway car. I suppose I could say that I want to go to the library with her after her teacher workshop, and then make a break for the train station while she's *in* the workshop. But that would make her look bad.

And even if I did come up with a good excuse, Mom and Gabe would never let me go after what happened this morning. I'm grounded. Maybe this isn't such a great idea.

But as hard as I try, I can't shake the thought of ditching Gabe and starting new. Of course, I'd miss Mom, but it would be for her own good. Maybe if I leave, she'll dump Gabe, too, and give him those two kids as good-bye gifts. Then she could move to Brooklyn. She and Dad wouldn't have to get remarried—even I know that would be a bad idea. We could all just live in the same neighborhood and be almost like a real family.

I grab my reader's journal from my desk and start reviewing all the notes I wrote about whales. Not sure why. Guess I don't like the thought of ditching Rosie along with everyone else. But what's the point? She isn't gonna be making me famous anytime soon.

I throw the journal across the room. It bounces off the wall and lands on the floor face-up, wide open, right next to a pile of laundry. And I just stare at it because I have nothing else to do. I stare at it. Stare at it and think some more. Think until another idea hits, an even better one. One that guarantees a first-class ticket out of here.

I jump up from the beanbag chair and grab the journal. Then I go to my desk, find a pen, and pull the essential ingredient from my dictionary: a sick note that Mom wrote for me last year, after that bad case of poison ivy. Turned out Mrs. Heaney never asked for it, so I tucked it away for a rainy day. And here it is, a rainy day. Sunniest rainy day of my life.

I tear a piece of paper from my journal and place it over the sick note. When I think of just the right thing to say, I adjust my lamp so that the bulb is shining full force onto the paper. And I begin writing.

# Chapter Ten

# The Last Straw

*Monday evening, August 21st*

I've been grounded now for almost a day and, you know, it isn't so bad. I went to tutoring, made popcorn, then built that *Titanic* model Ted gave me when the movie came out. And now it's almost time for dinner. Mom ordered Chinese, my favorite kind of take-out. She agreed to hold off serving it until the end of the game show I'm watching. Not so bad at all.

Of course, it helped that Leslie fell for my plan—hook, line, and sinker. She didn't even bat an eye when I handed her the note. She just nodded her head, said "I'll meet you there," and tucked it into her notebook. Smooth.

OK, I admit it feels kind of weird knowing that I won't be living here after Saturday. There are things I'll miss, like my trophies and CD player. And people, like Kate and Aunt Louise and, of course, Mom. But it's time to move on. I can have my stuff sent to me once I get settled in Brooklyn. People can visit. Things will be fine once I get settled.

Still, it's hard to look at Mom and Gabe without thinking, if you only knew. If you only knew that in five short days, you'll have a spare bedroom. You'll have the good TV all to yourselves. You'll only need take-out for two. For a change, *your* lives will be flipped upside down. In five short days. If you only knew.

"Justin, dinner," Mom calls.

I turn off the TV and go to the table. Gabe is already sitting there, silent. I feel like telling him to get over it, but figure I'm in deep enough already. Why make matters worse? So I just plop down and start in without saying anything. See, two can play his game.

Mom spoons steamed vegetables from one of the white take-out boxes onto her plate and then hands them to me. I say, "Thanks, but no thanks," and go for the fried rice. Gabe just sits there gnawing on a sparerib, staring at me like I'm a sideshow freak. So I stare right back like he's one, too.

Mom tries to make nice. "How was tutoring today?"

"Good."

"What did you learn?"

I hate that question. In my book, it belongs in the Annoying Question Hall of Fame, right alongside "Have you cleaned your room yet?" and "Did you give your aunt a kiss good-bye?"

But I don't want to create any more waves so close to my escape, so I tell Mom what she wants to hear. "I learned how to question the author."

"Really?" she gushes.

"Yep." I flash her a big, big smile.

"Tell me more about it," she says.

"Well, when you're reading, right?"

"Right."

"You stop every now and then and think about what you're thinking. And if you have any questions, you ask them to the author because he's the guy who put the ideas down in the first place."

Gabe grumbles something that I don't hear.

Mom keeps going. "But how can you ask the author questions? It's not like he's sitting right there next to you."

"Well, you're supposed to ask the question, keep it in your head, and see if he answers it later in the book. Get it? See, Leslie says reading is not just about getting the words right. It's about understanding. That's why you ask questions."

"Then I'm really lucky," says Mom.

"What do you mean?"

"I have questions about a piece of writing, and the author is sitting right here."

I turn to Gabe, wondering if he got a book contract or something. But that's impossible. He can barely write his name. I turn back to Mom. "I don't get it."

Then she pulls the forged note from her shirt pocket . . . and I get it. Boy, do I get it.

"While you were in your room working on your

model today, Leslie stopped by and gave me this," she says, holding the note up between her thumb and index finger.

Suddenly I feel like I'm about to lose all the fried rice I just ate. How could Leslie have done this to me? I trusted her. Guess it doesn't matter at this point. I try to think of a way out. "Where did she get that?" I ask.

"Not sure," Gabe answers. "It's signed by your mom, but she claims she didn't write it. Now who could've?" He lifts his eyebrows like a bad actor. "I wonder."

If their goal is to make me squirm, they're doing a good job. Could I possibly be in deeper trouble? "Beats me," I say, as if it's going to help my cause.

"Let me read it to you. Maybe that will help you figure it out." Gabe takes the note from Mom and starts reading.

" 'Dear Leslie: I give Justin permission to ride with you to Boston this Saturday. Please pick him up at the school at 7:00 and drop him off at the Children's Museum, where he will meet his friend, Kate, and her father. He is staying with them in Boston until Sunday evening.' And then—here's the best part—it's signed with your mom's name."

The words float there for a few seconds waiting to be replaced by someone else's. But no one talks, including me. I can't think of an excuse. Maybe that's because I've used them all up. "How did Leslie know I wrote it?"

"And how did I know where you were this morning?" askes Gabe, icicles dripping from his words. "Those aren't the issues. You lied about the fishing equipment.

You forged your mother's name. You almost killed yourself on the boat. *Those* are the issues, Justin. Use your head."

Mom tries to bring the tension down a few notches. "Why Boston?" she asks, placing her hand on mine.

"I wanted to go to the museum with Kate," I lie. That's how much I can't stand Gabe. I'll lie as much as I have to, even now, if it means getting away from him on Saturday.

"Honey, that's not true," says Mom. "According to Brenda, Kate's not staying with her dad this weekend."

Suddenly everyone's silent, but not like earlier in the conversation. Not like they're waiting for me to spill my guts or anything. No, it's a different kind of silence. One that seems like it might not end, which scares me even more than getting caught on the boat, because, for the first time, it feels like they've given up on me. Like no matter what they ask, I'll lie. So why bother?

I sit there pushing uneaten water chestnuts around my plate, feeling tired all of a sudden. Really tired. "Can I go to my room?" I ask.

"Go," Gabe answers.

# Chapter Eleven

# The Conquest

*Tuesday morning, August 22nd*

Remember how I was talking about how weird sleep is? Like, most nights I sleep all the way through, but some nights I don't sleep at all and some nights I fall asleep right away, but then a bad dream wakes me up? Well, last night something different happened. I was awake until about four o'clock in the morning, and *then* I fell asleep. I was awake coming up with other escape plans, since my first one went down in flames. Thinking about blowing this clambake and starting a whole new life, with no Gabe, no twins, no teachers waving books in front of my nose and expecting me to beg for a chance to read. That would be great. That is, I thought it would be, last night before falling asleep.

Now it's seven. I'm still in bed, but I'm thinking less about running away. Don't get me wrong, I still hate Gabe and all, but I've reached the conclusion that coming up with another scheme could be one big waste of time. After last night's skirmish, security around here is going to be tighter than Alcatraz. I won't be going *any*where.

So here I am with absolutely nothing to do—me, the kid who was going to unlock the secrets of the universe. What a joke. It's strange to have nothing to do, no one to see, nowhere to be except alone with myself. I'm just staring at the ceiling, making pictures from the cracks by connecting them in my mind. I've gotten pretty good at crack pictures, actually. All it takes is a little imagination. Like those cracks in the corner. Are they forming the letter Q? Or a man sticking out his tongue? It's hard to tell.

I hear somebody outside, so I climb out of bed and go to the window. It's the warden organizing his fishing equipment on the lawn. He's got everything all lined up: rods, tackle box, cooler. Seems strange for a Tuesday morning, but like I said, he's obsessed with that stuff. Probably just wants to spend a little quality time with it before work.

I think about climbing back into bed, about staying there all day, but then I remember Mom bought a new box of cereal yesterday with a free plastic spoon inside that changes from red to green when you dip it into the milk, so I head downstairs in my pajamas to get it. Am I a loser or what?

Just as I hit the bottom of the staircase, Gabe walks through the front door. He looks a little less tired than he did last night, but just as angry. "Why aren't you dressed?"

I pretend I didn't hear him and make a bee-line for the cereal, which I can see sitting on top of the refrigerator.

"Justin, I asked you a question."

I stop and answer without looking at him. "Why should I get dressed? It's not like I need to be anywhere."

"I'm afraid you do," he says in a cold voice. But that doesn't scare me. Nothing scares me, except that silence he and Mom shot me at the end of dinner last night.

"Where? Reform school?" I answer.

Gabe looks at me as if that's an idea he hadn't considered but probably should've. "That's not what I had in mind," he says, in a slightly nicer voice. What *is* he up to?

"So where?"

"We're going fishing."

"Excuse me?"

"Go put on your smelly lucky shirt. We're going fishing." He speaks with such urgency, as if a meteor's about to blow the house away, that I don't ask questions. I just do what he says. I run upstairs, get dressed, and meet him in the driveway.

"I thought I was grounded."

"You are," Gabe says, handing me the rods and motioning toward the car.

"Don't you have to go to work?"

"No. Not today."

Suddenly I get nervous because I think of a movie I saw once where the bad guy, posing as a good guy, takes the *real* good guy out on a boat and dumps him overboard.

"You're not going to throw me overboard or anything, are you?"

"No. Not today." He passes me the tackle box and the cooler, and then he goes into the garage.

"So why are you taking me fishing?" I shout

to him through the big wooden doors. "I'm grounded, for two weeks, remember?"

Gabe comes out carrying the three garden rakes, still all rigged up with the ropes and lines and lures that Kate and I attached to them. "We've got a sea monster to catch."

It's confirmed: the man is crazy.

"I'm not getting in a boat with you."

"Why not?" he asks, looking at me like *I'm* the crazy one.

"Lately you are either screaming at me or giving me the silent treatment, and now all of a sudden you want to go fishing for a sea monster?" I ask him. "That doesn't seem a little strange to you?"

He thinks about it. "Get in the car."

It could be the biggest mistake of my life, but I follow his order. We drive back to Harrison's, park in the municipal lot, and unload. Gabe doesn't say much along the way, just a few comments about the weather and the sailing conditions. This makes me even more nervous. Why is he suddenly being so nice to me?

We head down the walkway, Gabe carrying the chunky stuff, like the tackle box and video camera, and me the skinny stuff, rods and rakes. When we get to slip seven, he climbs aboard *The Beast*, puts everything down and signals for me to hand him the rest of the things I'm carrying.

Our eyes meet for the first time all morning, making the situation even more confusing than it already is. I want answers, so I ask him in all seriousness, "Why are you doing this?"

He looks away. "I want to help you catch the sea monster."

"No, really, why are you?"

He looks back at me, and I notice something that I haven't seen in awhile—his wise-guy smile, the one he'd flash when we'd talk about ant farms and dirt bikes and stuff. The one just for me, that said nothing else mattered but me. I'd forgotten about it.

"Because you're my son," he says.

Oh, please. What is this, a soap opera? I've heard enough.

"Problem is, you're not my real father."

The wise-guy smile disappears. "And you think that guy in Brooklyn *is?* "

"As a matter of fact, he is."

"But who raised you?"

"Mom did, and Aunt Louise. Grandpa and Grandma," I snap. "Not you." Suddenly I just want to be back in bed making pictures out of ceiling cracks.

Gabe closes his eyes tight like he's trying to squash whatever stupid things are flying around inside his head. "The whole point of taking you out today, Justin, was to talk," he says very slowly, very calmly. "Your mom and I are worried about you. You've been making some really bad decisions lately."

"Wouldn't have been so bad if I hadn't gotten caught."

Gabe looks at me like that's not the issue, but doesn't say it this time. I suppose he's right. I step onto the boat and loosen the rope from the piling. Gabe starts her up. We pull away from the dock, gradually picking up speed as we make our way past the sailboats anchored around the harbor. I feel the wind race through my hair, the sun beat down on my forearms, and the sea spray hit my face when we collide into another motorboat's wake. It's awesome, like each of those things—wind, sun, spray—is a part of me.

Once we make it through the channel, past the northern tip of Rose's Island and into open ocean, Gabe kills the engine.

"Hand me the rakes," he says.

"Do you really think this is going to work?" I ask.

"Well, I assume you did your homework."

I did, a ton of it. At least he's giving me credit for that.

He starts tying the ropes, the ones fastened to the rake handles, around the legs of the fishing seats in the stern. Then he untangles some of the lines hanging from the prongs and tests to make sure that the sardine lures have been tied nice and tight.

"You and Kate did a good job."

Must admit, he's making it difficult for me to hate him. "Do you think casting them out 20 feet is far enough?" I ask.

"Yeah, boat noise shouldn't bother anything at that distance."

I scan the water's surface. It's flat, all the way to the horizon. No sign of anything. "Do you really believe there's a sea monster out there—or are you just pulling some pop parenting psychology on me?"

Gabe gazes out to sea alongside me. "I want to believe there's one." And then he turns to me. "I really do." And he means it. I can tell because the wise-guy smile's back.

"Finally, you're talking sense," I tell him.

"Tell you what," he says. "I'll make a deal with you."

More deals. Why are the adults in my life so into making deals? I always wind up on the short end.

"What kind of deal?"

"I'll work on believing in sea monsters if you'll work on believing that we—me, you, your mom, and the twins—are a team. A family."

See what I mean about winding up on the short end? "I will if you will."

"What makes you think I won't?"

"In case you haven't noticed, all you do lately is yell at me. And maybe, if I'm lucky, tell me a stupid joke afterward to smooth things out. Other than that, all you talk about is the twins. Your real kids. If you think you're my father, act like him."

I'm not quite sure where that came from—maybe some holding tank deep inside.

Gabe looks at me like a dog that just got kicked. "I didn't realize I was doing that."

"All I want is equal time."

"Deal." Gabe starts up the engine. When we reach about 15 miles an hour, he gives a thumbs-up. I throw out the first rake. It bounces sideways when it hits the water and then pushes back to the full length of the rope. Then I throw the second one out. Then the third. Within minutes, all of them are skipping along the surface, like water skis without skiers.

We spend the better part of the morning cruising around Shoal Ledge, a couple miles out, catching nothing but floating bundles of seaweed. At about noon, Gabe asks me if I'm hungry. I tell him yes, so he kills the engine again, and we break for the lunch he packed in the cooler.

We don't say much. Just sit there in the sun, munching on our tuna sandwiches, gazing out toward Gull Island, slowly accepting the fact that today probably isn't the day that the secrets of the universe make the front page.

I'm thinking about other stuff, too. Like how I've probably deserved to have Gabe mad at me most of the time. Like how I never used to lie—at least not about important stuff. I'm wondering if he and Mom will ever trust me again.

"Gabe," I say into the comfortable silence, "I'm sorry I've been acting like such a jerk."

"I know, champ," he says. "We both have things we're sorry for, I guess. It's what we do from here on that matters."

I nod, thinking that he makes a lot of sense for someone who's always joking around.

Then, all of a sudden, Gabe springs up like a hornet stung him. "What's that?"

I look where he's looking, but see nothing. "What?"

He points. "That."

We focus on the same spot.

And I see it: a curved piece of shiny brownish-blackish something, poking out of the water about 50

feet from the boat. I rise from my seat slowly, without taking my eyes off it, as if a sudden move, even a quick glance in the other direction, will scare it away. I'm not sure what it is, but the thought of it being a sea monster is too much for me to take. "Just a piece of driftwood. An old buoy maybe."

"It's moving," says Gabe.

It is moving, for sure, but on its own or because of the waves hitting it? I'm not sure, so I keep staring. And then it seems to poke itself up a little further and turn. It turns and looks right at us! And I see them. At least, I think I see them: watermelon eyes. Or are they just knots? Hard to tell, so I decide they're watermelon eyes. They're *definitely* watermelon eyes.

"Get the camera," I shout.

Gabe starts taping. We watch for five minutes.

Maybe more, maybe less. Hard to tell. We watch—him through the camera, me through bare eyes—whatever it is bob in and out of the water, rotating toward us and then away, as if it's as unsure about us as we are about it.

"Should we try to get closer?" Gabe asks.

"I think so."

He starts up the engine and points the boat in what-ever-it-is's direction. But the moment we move forward, it disappears into the purple-blue. Gone for good.

We both stare at the empty place. "You *did* see what I saw, right?" I ask.

"I sure did."

I turn to him. "Was it a sea monster?"

"Yes, I do believe it was."

I look back out to sea to decide whether he's telling the truth. I decide that he is, so I tell him, "Then I think it was a sea monster, too."

Gabe presses the rewind button on the video camera. He gives me a big smile, puts his free hand on my shoulder, and squeezes. "And you've got the evidence to prove it," he says.

I do. All the evidence I need. For sea monsters—and for other things, too.